Books by Jack Fisher

Single Titles

Passion Relapse

Passion Relapse

ISBN # 978-1-78686-140-5

©Copyright Jack Fisher 2017

Cover Art by Posh Gosh ©Copyright 2017

Interior text design by Claire Siemaszkiewicz

Totally Bound Publishing

This is a work of fiction. All characters, places and events are from the author's imagination and should not be confused with fact. Any resemblance to persons, living or dead, events or places is purely coincidental.

All rights reserved. No part of this publication may be reproduced in any material form, whether by printing, photocopying, scanning or otherwise without the written permission of the publisher, Totally Bound Publishing.

Applications should be addressed in the first instance, in writing, to Totally Bound Publishing. Unauthorised or restricted acts in relation to this publication may result in civil proceedings and/or criminal prosecution.

The author and illustrator have asserted their respective rights under the Copyright Designs and Patents Acts 1988 (as amended) to be identified as the author of this book and illustrator of the artwork.

Published in 2017 by Totally Bound Publishing, Think Tank, Ruston Way, Lincoln, LN6 7FL, United Kingdom.

No part of this book may be reproduced, scanned, or distributed in any printed or electronic form without permission. Please do not participate in or encourage piracy of copyrighted materials in violation of the authors' rights. Purchase only authorised copies.

Totally Bound Publishing is a subsidiary of Totally Entwined Group Limited.

If you purchased this book without a cover you should be aware that this book is stolen property. It was reported as "unsold and destroyed" to the publisher and neither the author nor the publisher has received any payment for this "stripped book".

PASSION RELAPSE

JACK FISHER

Dedication

To my family, my friends, and all those who supported
me.
From the bottom of my heart, I thank you.

Chapter One

'Hello. My name is Mary Ann Scott and I am a sex addict.'
Eleven months ago, a beautiful young woman named Mary had stood up in front of a crowd of strangers and said those fateful words for the first time. The young woman, who had once taken so much pride in being outgoing, loving and passionate, had spoken those words with such fear and uncertainty. Now a shadow of her former self, Mary sat quietly, listening, as just another misguided soul in the Hartman County Community Center.

"Hello. My name is Susan Michaels and I'm a sex addict," said a middle-aged woman.

"Hi, Susan," the crowd of similarly damaged attendees replied.

"I'm proud to say that it's been exactly one year since I've joined this program—a full year since I hit rock bottom. I thought I would never pull myself together after two divorces, five affairs and...I don't even remember how many one-night stands. But I did it. And it's all thanks to this great program and to you, my wonderful friends."

Susan received an extended round of applause. Some stood up and clapped while she beamed with pride. She looked way too happy for someone who had been in this program just a little longer than Mary. She couldn't possibly be this seemingly content.

Mary still gave her weak applause. A few came up to shake Susan's hand and give her a hug. Mary remained in her seat, keeping to herself and hoping she could stay invisible for the rest of the meeting. At one point, she had to look away. Susan's beaming success—however real it might be—only reminded her of her utter lack of progress.

"It's not fair. It's just not fair," Mary said under her breath.

She hugged her shoulders and kept her head down while everyone else congratulated Susan. As Mary looked around the room, she recalled the many lurid stories she'd heard since joining this program. The Chapman Hill Addiction Outreach Program—or CHAOP, as everyone called it—billed itself as the best addiction treatment program in the state. It had resources for every kind of addiction—from substance abuse to gambling and eating disorders. They didn't advertise the division that specialized in sex addiction, but it made the same bold claims, promising it could help men and women whose unhealthy sexual habits had destroyed their lives.

After nearly a year, however, that promise rang hallow. Sure, the program had helped Mary rebuild her life but only to a point. It might be less destructive than her previous life, but CHAOP didn't fulfill her in the ways the program had promised.

Susan Michaels might have been a lightweight in terms of her addiction, so maybe she'd had it easier. Affairs and one-night stands barely scratched the surface of what Mary had done. While she could hardly call herself the most decadent person in this program, she still felt *stuck* while everyone around her seemed to be making progress.

"Thank you. Thank you all," said Susan, now in tears.

She looked like she had just won the Super Bowl. Everyone in the room kept cheering for her, supporting her for her accomplishment. Mary still questioned just how much praise this woman deserved.

Over the past months, she'd heard about every kind of tragic story caused by sexual addiction. Men talked about how they had bankrupted themselves spending all their money on strip clubs, prostitutes and porn. Women talked about how they'd destroyed their lives by sleeping with their teachers in high school, seducing police officers and attending wild sex parties that had begun in one city and ended in another. Some of those acts had even resulted in prison time. Mary felt lucky in some respects, because she'd never ended up broke or in prison, but that luck only went so far.

Is that how I'm supposed to feel after a year? she wondered. *If so, I'm way behind.*

Mary tried to remain engaged, if only to avoid unwanted scrutiny. She watched her fellow addicts walk up to Susan to congratulate her. None of them appeared as conflicted as she was. Then again, she had a hard time relating to any of her peers.

It shouldn't have been a problem. These men and women came from many different walks of life. Some were young and attractive, not unlike the crowd Mary used to run with. Others were older and average-looking, the kind who nobody gave a second glance. From former strippers to retired accountants, they all had their own tragic story to tell. They each seemed to get something out of this, but Mary might as well have been an alien to these people.

What am I doing wrong? Why is Susan freakin' Michaels making so much progress while I'm stuck after almost a year? Am I missing something here or am I supposed to be this miserable?

No matter how many times she asked herself those questions, she never got an answer. It didn't make sense. It also frustrated her to no end.

"You're awfully quiet this evening, Mary—more so than usual," said a familiar voice.

"Sorry, Sister. It's been a rough week for the fitness industry, what with droughts and heat waves keeping people indoors," replied Mary, avoiding eye contact as best she could.

"Your lying skills haven't improved much, either. I thought we agreed you would at least try harder to not brush off my concerns."

"Guess I forgot," muttered Mary.

"I'm sure you'll remember next time. Until then, why don't we save ourselves the trouble and discuss them?

We don't have to share them with the group. This can be another one of those conversations that stays between us."

Mary shook her head and groaned. Sister Angela had a heart of gold, but she could be downright annoying when it came to having uncomfortable conversations. She claimed to be a former sex addict, calling her younger self an unrepentant sinner of the worst kind.

She told very personal — and very graphic — stories about her descent from being a talented actress to becoming a drug-addicted prostitute in Los Angeles. Some of her experiences made Mary's problems seem like child's play, especially the ones that involved oil wrestling and rooftop orgies. Mary sometimes questioned their validity. But even if only half of those stories were true, it made her uniquely qualified for this program.

Now a middle-aged woman working closely with the Hartman Catholic Church, Angela Murphy said she'd found God after surviving a drug overdose. She claimed to be living proof that anyone could overcome their addiction. Having since taken a vow of chastity, she claimed her life had become so much richer. She made it seem so appealing. However, Mary found it difficult to get excited.

"Come on, Mary. You know you can tell me anything. I won't judge," the nun chided as she sat down in the chair next to Mary's.

"You *never* do," Mary conceded.

"Then say what you need to say. You don't have to tell me everything — just whatever makes you feel most comfortable."

"Funny, I remember a number of guys telling me that exact same thing before we took our clothes off."

"You're not laughing, so it can't be *that* funny. You're not known for your sense of humor, either, so I assume something is really bothering you."

"You know me too well, Sister," Mary said.

"I know you like to avoid your problems until they blow up in your face," Sister Angela said. "You've been hurt before because of that."

"You don't need to remind me."

"Then I also don't need to remind you how much worse it could've been if you'd kept avoiding your problems. So why take a chance?"

Sister Angela reached over and consoled Mary with a gentle pat on her shoulder. This made it next to impossible for her to brush the nun off again. She was just too damn kind. It annoyed Mary no end, but it didn't make the older woman's words less valid.

"Look at her. Look at how happy she is," Mary said, now gazing back toward Susan.

"She should be. She's come a long way," Sister Angela said.

"I still remember all the times she came to meetings looking like a wreck. I remember how she broke down in tears, talking about how she'd once banged every guy on her block while her husband was traveling. It wasn't that long ago that she'd claimed she couldn't control her urges—that she was always going to be an addict."

"She's not the first person to say that. She's not even the *hundredth*."

"I don't doubt that, but it doesn't even matter in the end because some way, somehow, she turned herself around and became this ray of virgin sunshine. It doesn't happen overnight, but it doesn't always happen over a lifetime, either," Mary said.

"It's a process. It can't be rushed or forced, but when it works...it's the healing power of God at its best," Sister Angela replied.

"And I've seen that healing power find so many others since I've been here. It's like every other week, someone has this epiphany—this realization that allows them to cure their addiction."

"Addiction can't be cured. It can only be treated."

"I know, damn it. And no, I'm not going to apologize for cursing."

"You rarely do. I've stopped expecting you to," Sister Angela said.

"And why should I?" scoffed Mary. "Because no matter what I do—no matter how hard I try—that healing power never finds me."

Mary's frustration got the better of her. That tended to happen whenever she talked to Sister Angela about her progress in the program or lack thereof. She didn't like arguing with a nun, but eleven months of inner turmoil made it difficult to stay calm.

Sister Angela still didn't hold it against her, although it might have been easier if she had. Mary kept hugging her shoulders, avoiding eye-contact, even while Sister Angela consoled her. The nun was so patient and understanding, making it very difficult to stay mad at her. She always let Mary vent when she needed to. On a day like today, she needed to do more than that.

"I just...don't know how much longer I can feel like this," Mary continued. "I've already uprooted my old life. I've put as much distance as I can between myself and everything that fueled my addiction."

"Do you regret that decision?" Sister Angela asked.

"No. It was hard but it was the right decision at the time," answered Mary. "It just left me feeling so...so broken. I thought coming back to my hometown and being part of this program would help me heal, but..."

She still couldn't articulate all the ways she had struggled since coming to terms with her addiction. She had given up trying. She honestly didn't think she could've felt this pathetic with her clothes on.

"A part of you still misses it," said Sister Angela, finishing the thought Mary didn't dare to complete.

"Misses what? The reckless sex? The endless indulgence? All the connections I used to enjoy, both personally and physically? The success, recognition and adulation of everyone around me? Why would anyone miss *that*?" Mary said, her every word dripping with sarcasm.

"It was a big part of your life. An addiction always is. That's what makes it an addiction. Your ability to walk away from it is a testament to your strength. But no matter how strong you are...walking away from something like that is going to leave a void."

Only Sister Angela could make an act of strength seem so weak. Mary sure didn't feel stronger after leaving her former sex-addicted ways. In many respects, getting away from a life of decadence and recklessness was an act of fear rather than strength. The fear had plagued her since she'd entered this program and she hadn't found the strength to overcome it, despite all her genuine effort.

"Is this the part where you tell me I should fill that void with the loving light of Jesus and become a chaste nun like you?" Mary said, her sarcasm not waning.

"Only if I were a less pious nun who didn't listen to the plight of sinners," said Sister Angela in a humorous tone. "Except I *have* listened and I understand that what works for one addict doesn't always work for another. My faith and my piety helped me fill that void. You might need something different."

"Like what? What could I possibly find that'll make me feel less...unsatisfied, if that's the right word?"

"I don't know, Mary. The program never claims to give addicts the solution. It only offers to guide them."

"Then I guess some addicts are just slower than others," Mary said.

"It's not about being slow. Some just need to find a different path," said Sister Angela. "For what it's worth, I think you're still on the right one. You *will* overcome this. You *will* find what you're looking for. You just need to have faith."

She makes it sound so easy.

That was what everybody in this program said in some form or another—have faith that it'll all work out. The advice may have helped them, but for some reason, it did her little good.

"When you say it like that, you remind me why I'd make a lousy nun," Mary said, with much less sarcasm this time.

"You and most other women, regardless of addiction," said Sister Angela in good humor.

"I just don't know how much more faith I can have at this point...or how much longer I can have it. Is it even possible that I'll figure it out by the end of the month? Believe me when I say I'd *love* to stand up there like Susan and proclaim I've turned a corner."

"I do believe it's possible. You're a beautiful young woman, Mary. You've got a great head on your shoulders. A lot can happen in a month. You just have to have faith and be ready when the time comes."

Mary remained skeptical, but still took comfort in Sister Angela's kind words. She didn't brush the nun off when she patted her shoulder again. Sister didn't even ask her to congratulate Susan. Sister was okay with Mary keeping to herself and staying on her own path, even though it left her so conflicted.

Sister Angela gave Mary one more reassuring smile before getting up to lend Susan her support. The nun's understanding came as a relief, but it only went so far. It still didn't feel like any part of her — body or soul — had been healed by this program. Mary was still so empty. Even after all this time, she still hadn't gotten used to the feeling.

She watched Sister Angela give Susan a hug while others continued to offer their support and congratulations. It went on way too long, but much to Mary's relief, the meeting was almost over. Susan may not have been a former model who'd once stopped traffic while crossing the street in a bikini, but she definitely looked more radiant now than Mary had in years.

Mary ended up looking away again, turning her attention to the glossy floor of the community center. In her reflection, she couldn't see the beautiful young woman Sister Angela had just mentioned.

"You have a great head on your shoulders and a beautiful

body. How can you possibly be this miserable?" she asked herself.

Mary had once taken so much pride in her body. Whenever she looked in the mirror, she didn't see some girl next door or some silicone-laden porn star. She saw someone who had worked long and hard to refine the natural beauty she'd been blessed with.

The woman she'd been had spent hours a day in front of that same mirror, smothering herself with overpriced makeup and fixing her hair so that it had a perfect, wavy sheen. And after she'd finished refining her complexion, she would have scoured her vast wardrobe for the perfect attire to complement her looks.

That attire had often included undersized tank tops, shorts that barely qualified as shorts and every kind of thong underwear in existence. If it hadn't shown an obscene amount of skin, then she hadn't bothered wearing it. No matter how revealing it had been, that version of Mary Ann Scott had worn it with pride. Because of this confidence, she'd seemed destined to be the hottest thing to ever come out of Hartman County. However, that woman didn't exist anymore.

"Maybe a better question is…how the hell did I let my problems ruin me so completely?" Mary said, still talking to her reflection.

She gazed at herself with bitter disappointment. Mary no longer saw the sexy, stunning woman once destined to grace the cover of every fitness magazine. She saw a woman who'd lied to herself about her problems and had come dangerously close to letting them destroy her.

Being an aspiring fitness model had come with a long list of perks. The world went out of its way to cater to the whims of a beautiful young woman. Men had lined up to impress her, buying her drinks and offering her every comfort imaginable. Sure, it was shallow and unfair, but Mary hadn't cared. She'd taken advantage of it at every turn and made damn sure she'd enjoyed it. She'd just taken it *way* further than she should have.

Now the woman she saw in the mirror bore all the burdens that Mary had ignored for too long. This version of Mary Ann Scott didn't spend hours getting ready for her day. She didn't spend a good chunk of her paycheck on overpriced makeup and hair conditioner. Instead, she only used eye-liner and lipstick that she bought from Walmart. On top of that, her clothes might as well have come from a second-hand store.

Nothing about her was overt anymore. Everything that had once made her so passionate and outgoing had collapsed under the weight of her reckless indulgences. Sex addict or not, she had to live with those choices.

Unable to bear the sight any longer, Mary closed her eyes and turned away from her reflection. She didn't come to these meetings to lament how far she had fallen. She came here in hopes of overcoming the addiction that had consumed her life. Those hopes were fragile, but she'd hung in for nearly a year now. She promised herself she would remain dedicated. She even believed on some level that she could find a way to fill the emptiness inside her, although that seemed increasingly unlikely with each miserable day that passed.

Accepting that she wouldn't find what she sought tonight, Mary stopped talking to herself and focused on the meeting. She might as well try to make something of it, even if it meant envying those who had.

"Thank you, Susan. And a special thanks to everybody who stood by her. Never forget that this is a collective effort. Addiction can overwhelm an individual, but it can never overwhelm a community bound by faith and emboldened by our Lord," said Sister Angela, who had returned to the front of the room.

"Amen, Sister!" said Susan, still basking in her accomplishment.

"It's also important to remember that you're never alone. We're here to support each other—to help one another.

Addiction leaves many scars and addiction to sex, in particular, tends to leave *unseen* scars. Some don't always heal, but everyone can find the strength to endure. That is the power of faith."

"Amen!" said several other addicts who had been supporting Susan.

This was the part of the meeting where Sister Angela reaffirmed the values and philosophy of CHAOP. She did it near the end of every meeting, so much so that Mary had memorized these mini-sermons to the letter. She still listened, but these moral lectures still didn't strike her as much as they'd obviously struck the Susan Michaels of the program. Mary began to wonder if the power of faith was enough for her.

"Now, before we leave for tonight, I want to open the floor to newcomers," said Sister Angela, continuing with the usual formalities. "We have a few new entrants to CHAOP, and it's still my policy to not require them to speak. I understand that the first meeting can be difficult, but for those who wish to share their story or just introduce themselves, this is your time to speak."

Sister Angela stepped aside and sat down, allowing anyone else to stand who dared to confess their addiction to a group of strangers. This was the part of the meeting where awkward silence slowed things down. Sometimes nobody did, ending the meeting on a mixed note. Mary would've preferred that. Then, much to her dismay, a tall man wearing a sweatshirt and a baseball cap stood and spoke.

"Hello. My name is Peter Robert Rogers," said the man.

"Hi, Peter," replied the crowd in perfect unison.

Mary immediately perked up at hearing that name. She rarely took an interest in newcomers to the program, but this name sparked one that went beyond her many problems.

"No. It can't be!" Mary said in disbelief.

She gazed at the man standing before a crowd of fellow addicts, scrutinizing every detail of his appearance. Her eyes told her one thing, but her brain told her something else. Mary kept listening, refusing to believe that fate would be this cunning.

"Um…I don't really know what to say here, so I guess I'll keep it simple," he said. "I was born right here in Hartman County. I left when I was fifteen. I just moved back this past weekend, and… Well, I am a sex addict."

Mary had to cover her mouth to keep from gasping in amazement. There might have been thousands of men named Peter Rogers in this world, but she knew of only one who had been born in this county, left at age fifteen and wore tattered baseball caps that any rational person would've thrown away years before. Eventually, she accepted what her brain told her, even if she didn't like the implications.

"My God…it's really him," Mary said under her breath.

She shook her head in disbelief. This was big. This posed more than a few questions about a part of her life that she barely remembered anymore. However, it might be worth recalling. If he was the same Peter Rogers, then her addiction had affected her even more than she'd thought.

Chapter Two

"Thank you for sharing your story with us tonight, Peter. It was very brave of you," said Sister Angela after hugging the program's latest entrant.

"Don't thank me yet, Sister. I'm...not in a good place right now. Don't expect me to be much braver than this—at least for the time being," Peter said.

"It's okay. Just being here and sharing your story is brave enough."

"Does that mean it gets easier?"

"Yes, but only to a point," said Sister Angela.

The nun rarely made such bold claims, a strange quality for such a pious woman. She told all newcomers that the Chapman Hill Addiction Outreach Program had high expectations but even higher commitments. Mary remembered Sister Angela describing those expectations and commitments after she'd joined. She imagined that Peter felt as overwhelmed as she had that first day.

"Overcoming an addiction requires more than just bravery," Sister Angela continued. "Given your situation, it may require more than most, but don't be discouraged. This program *can* help you. I'll see to it personally. I'll even pray, for good measure."

"Um...thanks," Peter said.

Sister Angela gave him one of the beaming smiles that made her so hard to argue with. She then stepped aside so she could talk to a few more people. The meeting had just ended and almost everyone had left already. There were always a few who lingered to chat or talk to Sister Angela about issues they couldn't share with the group.

Mary was rarely among those who stayed, but she'd made an exception tonight.

She'd kept her distance while Peter had talked to Sister Angela, but she had heard most of the conversation. She still couldn't believe it. The quirky, pudgy boy from a simpler time in her life had returned. However, he didn't look anything like she remembered.

He had changed a lot since the last time she'd seen him. She couldn't say the same about herself, but that only made her more eager to approach him after Sister Angela walked away.

"She rarely tells you what you want to hear, but she's honest in a way that grows on you...to a point," Mary said.

Peter turned around and looked at her strangely. He was taken aback at first, but then his demeanor shifted. He seemed to recognize her but apparently still needed a reminder.

"I'm sorry. Do I know you?" he asked. "You look... familiar."

"Fourth grade, Ms. Stintson's art class—the last day before the holiday break," replied Mary. "We were all painting posters, complete with sparkles and non-toxic paint. You set a tray of paint down on a chair to tie your shoe. Then Ms. Stintson sat down in the chair, ruined her special Christmas dress and pitched an epic fit. But before you raised your hand to confess, someone pulled you back and took the blame. If I recall, that same person had a nasty habit of borrowing your ChapStick and never giving it back."

He *had* to remember that story. They'd laughed about it for weeks after. Unless he'd completely purged his memories of his life in Hartman County, he had to realize who was standing in front of him. Peter blinked a few times in disbelief. Mary then stepped a little closer so he could confirm what she sensed he suspected.

"My God...Mary Ann Scott!" Peter said.

"Yes, Peter Robert Rogers. It's me," Mary said curtly.

"Wow. I, uh... You look... I'm sorry. I'm going to need a minute here," he stammered.

"Take all the time you need. It's not every day you meet an old friend in a sex addiction treatment program."

Just saying it out loud added to the awkwardness, but Peter still laughed. Addiction hadn't destroyed his sense of humor, it seemed. He also showed that he still had the winning smile that had made him such a lovable kid, but it was the only physical feature about him that remained unchanged.

"You're obviously not surprised by my looks, but I'm *definitely* surprised by yours," Mary said. "Are you really the same dorky kid I grew up with or did you undergo some radical body transplant?"

"There's nothing radical about it. I left before puberty did its thing. I guess you could say the growth spurt did wonders for my body and self-esteem," Peter said.

Mary took a step closer to get a better look at this growth. The Peter Rogers she'd known before and the Peter Rogers standing in front of her now might as well be two different people. In her memory, she still saw the pudgy, undersized boy that had grown up just a few houses down from her. He'd always had messy hair that he'd tried to cover with hats. He'd also had a pasty complexion that made every blemish stand out. He'd been physically unremarkable, but he'd never used it as an excuse to be the life of a party.

Now Peter needed no excuses. He had grown into a strong, fit and downright imposing young man. He stood nearly a foot taller than her and had a broad chest and well-developed arms. He didn't have the physique of a body builder, but he could easily be mistaken for an athlete, not unlike the ones she'd worked with during her days as a fitness model.

He even had the face to go with it, his pale complexion covered by a light beard surrounded by a layer of stubble. It was an undeniably masculine look from someone she'd never considered that masculine to begin with. Maybe she should have, because the boy she'd once known had become quite a man.

"Wonders indeed," Mary said as she reached out and touched his toned arms, "but puberty can't be the *only* reason for such a remarkable transformation."

"It's not. You should know, because you're one of those reasons — or did you forget your first success story as an aspiring fitness guru?"

"Not for a moment," Mary said. "Too bad neither of us could handle the success."

"So, you were listening to my confessions," Peter said.

"Among other things," she replied.

It got a bit awkward again, but Mary gave him a reassuring smile to salvage what remained of his ego. She didn't care about the details that had led him to this program. She was just content to talk to an old friend who'd known her before she'd screwed up her life so badly.

"Now I'm glad I chose my words carefully. There's...a lot I didn't say when I introduced myself," Peter said.

"That's okay. I didn't tell anyone my last name until my third meeting," Mary said.

"To be honest, I was tempted to spill my guts tonight. I've been through a lot of shit these past few months...to say nothing of everything that led up to it."

"I can imagine," Mary said.

"Between realizing that I'm a full-blown sex addict and finding out that I suck at treating myself, I'm not sure you can. I've dug myself into quite a hole. I'm also sure there are more than a few women who would love to bury me in that hole."

"I take it back. I can't imagine it anymore."

"Then I guess we're partially even. I can easily imagine you getting addicted to sex, even before I left. I just can't imagine you letting it become a problem," Peter said.

"Thanks...I think."

It remained awkward, but not enough to stop Mary from smiling. She had confronted some harsh realities since joining the program, just as she had confronted numerous ones after realizing she was a sex addict. There was something refreshing about Peter's honesty. She needed that at a time like this.

By now, almost everyone had left. Sister Angela had said her goodbyes to the remaining participants. Mary still had a lot of questions, and for once, few of them pertained to sex addiction.

"Mind if I get serious for a moment?" she asked him.

"You're welcome to try. I don't know how much more serious we can get in an addiction program," Peter said.

"I'll give it a shot. You see, I didn't come here expecting to reconnect with someone I haven't seen in a decade. To be brutally honest, lately I've been coming to these meetings mainly out of desperation."

"Desperation is usually a bad sign for a sex addict."

"That goes without saying," Mary said. "I've been with this program for almost a year now. Don't get me wrong. It's done a lot of good, getting me through some really dark moments. But over the past few months, I feel like I've... stagnated."

"That's not too encouraging for a newbie like me. You sure you wouldn't rather talk to someone who's licensed to handle this?" Peter said.

"Believe me, I've talked to those people...more times than I care to recall. Right now, I need to talk to someone who knows me as something other than a recovering sex addict."

Now it was Mary's turn to feel awkward. She used to never feel that way around men. A year ago, she could have just shown some cleavage to get what she wanted. This time, she sought something that cleavage alone couldn't get her. And right now, Peter Rogers was the only man who could give it to her.

"Tell me, Peter. Did you have any plans after this meeting?" Mary asked, probably doing a poor job of hiding her anxiety.

"Well, my original plan was to endure my first meeting, go

home and recover with the help of a six-pack and Netflix," Peter said. "Are you asking me to change those plans?"

"Only if you don't need to recover that badly," Mary said. "That pizza place we used to hang out in is still open. I was hoping we could catch up over a slice and a—"

Peter raised his hand and cut her off. Now he looked just as anxious she felt.

"Are you sure that's a good idea, Mary?" he questioned. "Doesn't this program have a policy against that sort of thing?"

"What kind of *thing* are you talking about?" Mary asked.

"You know what I mean. A pretty young woman and a vulnerable young man, who just happen to be a couple of recovering sex addicts... Do I need to go any further?"

He gave her a strange look that allowed Mary to fill in the blanks. She tensed at the implications, fighting the urge to slap him for assuming such a motive. She ended up sticking both hands into her pockets to hide her dismay.

He'd made a valid point. While a part of her still saw the same dorky boy she'd grown up with, she also couldn't deny that the man standing before her was very attractive. Had she not known him, she would've been tempted to flirt with him, letting some of those old, addictive habits of hers re-emerge. However, that exact reason might be why she needed this.

"I know what you're saying. I want to be really pissed at you right now so I can storm off. That would probably be easier," Mary said.

"So, what's stopping you?" Peter asked.

"For one, the alternative is going back home and spending the rest of the night being both pissed *and* miserable. And if it's all the same to you, I'd rather not do that."

"Can't say I blame you," he conceded.

"The other thing is—" Mary had to stop herself mid-sentence. She struggled to put into words what she hoped to gain here.

"I think you just made my point," he said as he turned to

22

leave. Her hesitancy had obviously added to his reluctance.

"Wait! Don't go," urged Mary, grabbing his wrist before he could walk away. Peter stopped where he stood. Now he looked uncomfortable. She must have seemed pathetic, a far cry from the confident girl he remembered. To his credit, he didn't walk away and he listened with genuine concern.

"I'm sorry. I just… It's been a while since I reached out to someone for both the right *and* wrong reasons," Mary said.

"Right *and* wrong?" questioned Peter.

"Yes. Wrong in the sense that this program frowns on private meet-ups with the opposite sex, but right in the sense that I want to reconnect with a part of my life where I didn't have so many problems."

"It still sounds like we're tempting fate…among other things."

"Maybe we are, but at some point, we have to prove we can handle it," Mary said. "I know you are new in the process, but I'm coming up on a year in this program. I want— I *need* to show I've made some headway. And if you're going to make that same progress, who better to help you than the girl you once dared to eat worms?"

She'd made it sound more pragmatic than it really was, but Peter still laughed. It also helped hide how little Mary had thought this through. She had been overthinking a lot of her actions lately, often to the point of frustration. She needed to take a chance again. It might as well be now, with an old friend who understood the rigors of being a recovering sex addict.

"When you say it like that, I wish I had some worms with me," Peter said.

"Is that a yes or a no?" Mary said, rolling her eyes.

"It's a yes," he said. "Just promise me we'll pig out on greasy food and sugary soda in the least sexy way possible — you know, for good measure."

"Deal."

Chapter Three

A lot of things had changed in Hartman County over the past ten years, but Canicci's Pizza wasn't one of them. The place still made the best pizza in the state. It still operated out of the same ugly brick building along North Ridge Drive, just two blocks away from Mitchell Junior High School. That made it a popular after-school destination for generations of hungry students who couldn't stomach the cafeteria food. For Mary and Peter, it had been both a pit stop and a sanctuary.

Mary had left the community center feeling tense after her unexpected reunion with Peter. They'd ended up driving in separate cars to avoid any further awkwardness. Then, when they'd met outside, walked through the front door and smelled that distinct Canicci's Pizza aroma, Mary's tension had faded. After a couple of slices and a large soda, Mary almost forgot that she'd just come from a treatment program for sex addicts.

"Wow. I didn't realize just how much I missed this place until fifteen minutes ago," Peter said, his mouth still partially full. "I don't know what they served me in Los Angeles, but it sure as hell wasn't this good."

"Glad to hear the west coast didn't completely ruin your palate," Mary said, who still had half a slice left.

"It ruined a lot of things in my life, but my palate isn't one of them. That's not to say it didn't try. I guess I have a low threshold for kale, soy and organic salads."

"I don't care how health-conscious you are. Everyone needs something greasy and fattening to balance out their diet."

"Or just balance in general," Peter said. "I think you and I know the value of that better than most."

"More like we know the problems that come with being so *unbalanced*," Mary said.

Good food and fond memories had helped make the evening seem less arduous. Being a recovering sex addict gave Mary a strong appreciation for anything that distracted her from her problems, especially after a CHAOP meeting. A big part of the treatment involved finding new activities and outlets that guided addicts *away* from their addiction. This might not have been what Sister Angela had in mind, but it did the trick.

Reconnecting with an old friend from her childhood helped Mary feel less overwhelmed about her lack of progress. She didn't have many people from her past that she kept up with. There were many reasons for this and not all of them were good ones. Peter Rogers had somehow slipped through the cracks, and Mary felt lucky that of all the men it could have been, it had been him.

"So, tell me more about Los Angeles—well, minus the problems we know all too well," Mary said.

"What's there to tell? That's where I moved with my family after I left Hartman County. That's where I went to school, made new friends and set up a new life...until I ruined it, that is," Peter said.

"You've already told me the basics and you told everyone else back at CHAOP how you did that. I'm more interested in what happened in between."

"Interested because you're genuinely curious? Or interested because you don't believe the details?"

"Does it have to be one or the other?" retorted Mary. "You left Hartman County so suddenly. One day, I'm hanging out with my friend. The next, I hear you have three weeks to pack because you're moving to the west coast. And I don't remember getting an explanation beyond your dad getting a new job."

"Yeah, I guess I owe you an apology for that," Peter said

sheepishly.

"No, you don't. You were fifteen. You had no control over the situation. I was fourteen and had even less. We were too old to cry about it but too young to make sense of it. We were at that perfect age where we had a valid excuse for drifting apart."

"I miss having those kinds of excuses." He sighed.

"We all do. I also miss having someone who knew me before I started filling out bras and thongs. And I'd like to know what happened to my friend after I began my descent into addiction, so to speak."

For a moment, she sounded exactly like her younger, pre-addict self. She remembered being very upset when she'd found out that Peter was moving, so much so that she'd pushed him away to some extent. Now, after over a decade apart, Mary had a chance to make up for those poor decisions. Compared to the many she'd made later in life, it was minor at best, but any bit of progress helped at this point.

"Well, that friend didn't forget about you or the impact you had on him, so take comfort in that," Peter said.

"I do. Then again, my impact on you was never in doubt," Mary said coyly.

"Point taken," he said. "I needed that because I arrived on the west coast full of doubt. I didn't know what I wanted to be or how I would fit in. My parents sure didn't make it easy. They got so caught up in their careers that they left me and my sister to our own devices."

"It could've be worse," shrugged Mary. "How did your little sister handle it, anyway?"

"I'd...rather not talk about Britney. That's a very sore subject, and if it's all the same to you, I don't want to dwell on it."

"I understand completely. Dwell on whatever you feel comfortable with. The last thing I want to talk about is another sore subject." Part of her remained curious. Mary hadn't forgotten about Peter's sister, but she had never been particularly close to her. Having already taken a few chances tonight, Mary opted to focus on less melodramatic issues.

"There's a lot I can tell you about living on the west coast," Peter continued. "It's a very different world. Hartman County might as well be another planet by comparison. It was either going to eat me alive or make me stronger."

"If your biceps are any indication, I think it's clear who won the fight."

"And a big part of that is because of you," he said. "You remember how I was as a kid. I may have been adorable in the eyes of my parents, but I knew the truth. I was a walking can of pudge who would use *any* excuse to get out of gym class."

"I still remember the day you wrapped your toe in bandages and claimed it was broken. Good times," teased Mary.

"It worked, but those kinds of excuses don't cut it in a place like LA. It's a glitzy, glamorous town where everyone thinks they have what it takes to be the next big thing. I probably would've become bulimic if I hadn't met you. From the day we met until the day I left, you kicked my ass to get me motivated. You saw that I didn't like being a pudgy little dork. You went out of your way to help me do something about it."

He made it sound like she'd belittled him into bettering himself, but he'd shown how grateful he was that she'd done that. Mary remembered those days fondly, more so than he probably did.

"We couldn't have been more different," Peter said. "You were this adorable little tomboy who had so much energy. I honestly can't remember you hanging out with any girls. You preferred running around with the guys, proving that you could be as strong and as tough as them. And, unlike most of those guys, you *worked* for it."

"Just one of the many benefits of having two athletic older brothers," Mary said proudly.

"And you were all too eager to share those benefits. You got me off my ass and started working me out like a drill sergeant. You made me want to be stronger, faster and better. And whenever someone made fun of me for not being as fit, you had my back."

"Only because I liked picking fights," Mary said. "It got me into trouble, but it toughened me up."

"It toughened me up, as well. That's what made me more prepared than most when I moved to Los Angeles. I saw this glamorous world full of possibility. At the same time, I saw this overweight, dorky guy in the mirror. I decided early on that I was going to be better than that. I was going to use what you taught me to carve my place in that town. So, with all that motivation, I put in the work. The results? Well, I guess they speak for themselves."

Peter flexed his arms, showing off in ways he'd never dared to back when they had been kids. It was a testament to how much work he'd put into himself. He could've easily been competition during her days as a fitness model. All those fond memories of the boy she'd grown up with made the results even more impressive.

As much pride as he clearly had in that physique, however, Peter still looked conflicted. He paused for a moment to finish his soda. When he set it aside, he stared distantly at the table. By all accounts, he'd succeeded in overcoming the physical limitations he'd had as a kid. However, these obviously weren't the source of his problems.

"As I got older and puberty worked its magic, I became a walking California kingpin," Peter said. "I had the hair of a surfer, the body of an athlete and the competitive attitude of a Hollywood wannabe. It gave me so many advantages in high school and junior college, but what set me apart from the other pretty boys was how much I worked for it."

"In that sense, I think you earned the right to have an ego," Mary said.

"I did. And I'm not going to lie. I enjoyed it. I felt like I accomplished more than the other guys who had good genes or could afford a personal trainer."

"Sounds like you did. You deserved to enjoy it."

"And in a place like Los Angeles, the benefits are pretty damn sweet. You make a lot of good friends, meet a lot of hot girls and find a lot of nice job opportunities. I could've used those benefits in any number of ways. I still don't know how I ended up becoming a firefighter, but it was just one of those things that fell into place."

He didn't seem nearly as conflicted about that part of his life. He'd mentioned his job as a firefighter when he'd first introduced himself at the meeting. Mary remembered wondering what had led him down that career path, but it made sense.

Peter had always been a guy who'd felt like he needed to do something meaningful with his life. That was a big reason why he'd responded to Mary's efforts to whip him into shape as a kid. He could've done so many great things with a strong body and a tough work ethic. Saving people from burning buildings definitely qualified in her book.

"Whatever you call it, I think you did okay for yourself," Mary said. "Being a firefighter is way more respectable than my line of work."

"I don't know. The world needs fitness models and personal trainers, too," teased Peter.

"Not as much as it needs people willing to put their lives on the line for total strangers. That's a challenge that requires a whole different level of commitment."

"It also comes with a whole host of other benefits. You get respect from the community, a sense of accomplishment and skills you don't get in a classroom or an office. Then there's the camaraderie you feel with your fellow firefighters. That's something most people don't understand."

"Considering the cut-throat competition among models, I won't argue that," Mary said. "We'd sooner stab each other in the back than become friends."

"I guess it's a by-product of having to rely on one another," Peter said. "We didn't just work together. We had to live, train and fight fire together. You never know when you're going to get that call you might not come back from. Your best survival tool is often the guy standing next to you, so it helps that he really gives a damn."

The concept sounded so foreign to Mary. It really shouldn't have—a group of people establishing close personal bonds through their work and shared goals. It once again reminded her of the tough, callous world she'd come from and how it had nearly destroyed her.

She tried not to think too much about that. Every time she did, she got angry at herself for the choices she'd made. Peter had made very different ones that had put him in very different situations. However, he'd still ended up with the same problem—being an overwhelmed, overburdened sex addict who'd left everything behind. It only heightened her curiosity.

"Sounds pretty special," Mary said.

"It was," Peter said distantly.

"*Was*? Or still is?" she questioned.

"I know what I said. It means *exactly* what you think it means."

Now Peter looked to be the one getting angry with himself. He stared at his empty plate, gazing at his reflection. It seemed not unlike what she had done earlier with her reflection, seeing beyond the attractive surface and scrutinizing the problems that plagued him. She attempted to comfort him, but he didn't respond.

"All those benefits of being a firefighter helped make me a better man," Peter said. "They made me proud of what I did. The more I helped people, the more I wanted to get better at it. But among all those benefits, I let one of them ruin *everything*—one that didn't have to ruin *anything*. I guess that's where you can trace the origin to my current host of problems."

"We don't have to talk about them if you don't want to. You already told everyone the basics back at the meeting. There's no need to repeat them," Mary said.

"I told them about the extent of those issues. I didn't say anything about what caused them. There's a reason, and you might understand that reason better than most."

"How do you figure?" she asked.

"Because you also worked in an industry that had those benefits," he replied. "I don't want to assume, but I'm guessing you couldn't handle them, either."

It was a crude, shallow assumption—the benefits of being an attractive female fitness model carrying some very suggestive undertones. There was no judgment in his voice, but it still annoyed Mary to some extent. However, she couldn't argue with his logic.

"That's...not entirely wrong."

"Then I don't need to explain to you how being a hard-working, physically fit firefighter attracts a lot of women. Bear in mind that this was in Los Angeles. I'm not talking about soccer moms and Sunday school teachers. I'm talking about women who spend more on their tits than most people spend on their first car."

"I lived in Miami, less than a block away from South Beach. I think I can imagine," Mary said.

"You'd still only know half the story. It's the other half that nearly broke me." Peter tensed up again. He began cracking his knuckles and making fists while still staring at his reflection in his plate. He looked downright angry with himself but not for the same reasons as Mary. If his expression was any indication, it involved something much more personal than sex.

She briefly contemplated stopping him, but she chose not to. This was no longer about curiosity. Something really bad had happened to her friend and she had to know what.

"You still remember how I was before I left, don't you? Reserved, awkward and not nearly having enough confidence," Peter continued.

"I haven't forgotten," Mary said.

"Well, that didn't change as much as you'd think after I became an adult. Sure, I was this big, strong guy who wasn't afraid to work his ass off, but I was still reserved, to some extent. So, when all these beautiful women began throwing themselves at me? Well, it was pretty hard to refuse."

"No need to convince me. I know. Boy, do I know," Mary said, "and, yes, that means exactly what you think it means."

"It still says more about me than it says about you. I worked so hard to get bigger, stronger and better-looking. I worked so hard to get into a job that I felt passionate about. When the women entered the mix, it felt like I'd earned it. I just ended up taking way more than I'd earned."

"People tend to do that when they develop strong sexual appetites," Mary said, once again speaking from experience.

"My sexual appetite wasn't even half the problem," Peter said. "It wasn't enough to just have sex with these women. I had to do more. I had to be the man who satisfied every slut, bimbo and wannabe nymphomaniac in Southern California. Three-ways, parties, orgies, one-night stands... I would do whatever it took. I would put in the work, just as I had done before, and I assumed that so long as I played it safe, it wouldn't be a problem. Then...I screwed up in a way that will haunt me for the rest of my life."

At this point, he wasn't talking to her or anyone in particular. The look in his eyes indicated Peter was reliving that mistake in his mind. She knew that look, because she had seen it in herself before. It could only come from someone who'd had their world utterly shattered.

Not too long ago, Mary had experienced that same feeling. It had been so jarring that it had driven her from the successful, decadent life she'd once eagerly embraced. It had taken trauma of a special kind to make someone walk away from that world. She hadn't thought she would meet anyone who understood — until tonight.

In the eleven months since Mary had been treating her addiction, she had heard all sorts of crazy stories from other sex addicts. Too many of those stories were basic, built around similar themes like bad influences and poor impulse control. Her story had more complexity, so much so that she'd thought she was alone. Now, she was sitting across from a man who might actually share that burden.

"I'm sorry, Peter. I'm sorry you have to shoulder that pain," Mary said in an understanding tone.

"I'm the only one who should be sorry. I did it to myself," Peter said, dropping his head low.

"That doesn't mean you should torture yourself endlessly. You're already doing the right thing. You're treating your problem rather than ignoring it."

"It doesn't feel like I'm succeeding," he said.

"It takes time. And you don't have to go it alone anymore. I know exactly where you're coming from. I screwed up, too…every bit as badly as you did."

"I find that hard to believe."

"Humor me," Mary said. "You don't have to tell me what happened to you, but I'm willing to tell you what happened to me…if you're willing to listen. Maybe we can help each other through this. Maybe this is what we need right now — someone who can listen *and* understand."

As she said those words, Mary reached across the table and grasped Peter's hand in an affectionate manner. She didn't realize she had done it at first, but as soon she felt his tense grip, she gave it a warm squeeze to convey her sincerity.

Peter responded, squeezing back for a brief moment. They were fighting the same addiction. They also happened to be old friends. That should more than convince him that she meant what she said.

For a brief moment, he smiled back. Then, in an instant, his demeanor did a complete reversal. He pulled away from her grip and got out of the booth.

"No! Mary, I – This was a *bad* idea. I should *never* have agreed to this," Peter said, now shaking his head as if to clear it.

"What? What are you…?" Mary was taken aback. Peter acted like she'd just slapped him across the face. She got up as well, but he just took another step back.

"I know what this is, Mary. You might not see it, but I do," Peter said apprehensively. "You and me relating to one another — a couple of recovering sex addicts sharing their inner demons... It's a disaster waiting to happen. Your heart is in the right place, but it's the other parts of your body I don't trust."

She blinked a few times, having to digest what he'd just said. It didn't take long for her to process the implications behind his words. Those implications weren't just insulting. They were infuriating. Her confusion turned into outrage.

"You *asshole!*" shouted Mary.

"Don't be too offended. I don't trust parts of my body, either. One of them is already sending me some conflicting signs," Peter said, holding his hands up defensively.

"Still very offended," she said with folded arms. "Still *not* liking the assumptions you're making."

"That doesn't mean they're wrong. Don't tell me you didn't feel it, too. I'm just...not ready to deal with that yet. I want to overcome my addiction. I *want* to be better."

"You think I don't want the same?" she retorted.

"I don't know. Maybe you're looking for an excuse or something. Well, guess what? I can't be that excuse. I *won't.* You're just...going to have to find another way to deal with your problems. Assume whatever you want, but I need to leave."

Now avoiding eye contact completely, Peter left the restaurant as quickly as he could. He couldn't seem to get away from her fast enough, leaving Mary outraged and confused. Their exchange had caught the attention of other customers. They all looked at her strangely, not sure what they'd just witnessed. She wasn't entirely sure either, but it was enough to make her even angrier.

"What are *you* looking at?" yelled Mary.

Most of the other patrons wisely turned away. Still fuming, Mary stormed out. This once-promising evening was officially ruined. She'd thought she'd actually found someone who could help her with her problems. Instead, he'd become the latest in a long line of setbacks.

Chapter Four

"God damn fucking asshole of a friend! Who does he think he is, calling me an *excuse*? I should've kicked him in the balls!"

The steady stream of angry cursing came pouring out as soon as Mary left Canicci's Pizza. She barely remembered the drive back to her apartment, but she did remember running a stop sign and honking her horn twice while waiting at a traffic light. She was so pissed off about what Peter had said to her that she felt ready to take it out on anything that annoyed her.

Miraculously, Mary made it home without hitting anybody or getting pulled over, but she kept on fuming as she walked up to her apartment. She ended up slamming the door and throwing her purse across the room, knocking over a lamp in the process. She didn't even turn on the lights. She just paced around, venting her anger however she could.

She'd *thought* she'd done something important tonight. She'd *thought* she'd reached out and connected with someone in ways that didn't involve getting naked. It had felt way more meaningful than anything she had done with CHAOP lately. For a brief moment, all the frustration over her utter lack of progress had faded. It could've been a turning point. Instead, Peter had shattered it in the most infuriating way possible.

Now, Mary found herself back at square one. She might have even taken a step backward. In a fit of frustration, she opened her refrigerator and retrieved a half-empty bottle of wine. She didn't even get a glass. She just ripped the cork off and started chugging. She needed something to calm her down — or at least numb the pain of another failure. It wouldn't work as well as she wanted, but it still offered the shallowest kind of comfort.

"Fuck you, Peter! Fuck you for being so...so weak!" shouted Mary. "I thought you were my friend. Then you just cut and run because you can't stand being around beautiful women anymore? Fuck you!"

She gulped down most of the wine so fast that some of it dribbled down her face and stained her shirt. She didn't care, though. She was beyond that.

With the bottle still in hand, Mary leaned on her kitchen counter and sighed. The alcohol couldn't take effect fast enough, which might as well count as another fail. That seemed to be the only result she could manage lately.

Mary still wasn't accustomed this kind of failure. She had been used to getting what she wanted. Being a beautiful woman made things so much easier. If she didn't have the physical strength to do something, she could always rely on her outgoing personality to charm others into helping her. Even if that charm often involved reckless, meaningless sex, Mary still got her way.

Now, she genuinely *needed* something to help make her feel less broken. No matter what she did, she just couldn't get it and it was taking a toll on her.

"Fuck you! Fuck everyone! Nobody can help me. Nobody!" she yelled.

Mary took a few deep breaths, muttering more curses to vent her frustration. Eventually, her thoughts settled. Feeling defeated and pathetic, she looked down at her shirt to see the messy wine stain she'd created.

"Great. I just bought this shirt, too," she groaned.

Setting the bottle of wine aside for a moment, Mary pulled her shirt over her head and threw it across the room. She didn't bother getting another one. She was content to walk around in her bra for the rest of the night. Right now, she needed to focus on something that wouldn't piss her off.

Content to call the night a bust, she retrieved her wine bottle, just in case she still needed it. Then she stormed over to her couch and turned on her TV. At this point, she was the exact opposite of the sexy, glamorous personality who had once held South Beach in the palm of her hand. She felt like a bitter, burned-out bitch.

It seemed outrageous that an attractive woman in her twenties could be so miserable. Mary was living proof that even a woman like her could self-destruct in the least spectacular way possible.

"I swear if I see an ad featuring some sexy underwear model, I'm throwing my TV out the window," Mary muttered.

She drank more of her wine and began flipping through the channels, not caring about what was on. She just needed something simple and bland that wouldn't add to her frustration. Eventually, she settled on the evening news. Nothing there could *possibly* make her feel more pathetic.

"Recapping our top story, another rash of wildfires broke out at the Rock Hill Woodlands earlier today. Hartman County fire squads, as well as squads throughout the tri-county area, are still working to contain the spread. The ongoing heat wave is once again being cited as the primary cause. This adds to what has already been a record year for wildfires. The National Weather Service issued more warnings today that the trend may continue. We now go live to Rock Hill, where our crew has been on the scene all day."

Heat waves and subsequent wildfires happened all the time. This year just happened to be particularly bad. It was as if nature mirrored Mary's misery. She scoffed at such a thought and took another sip from her almost empty wine bottle.

She stopped listening to the reporter and just watched the scene unfold. A series of videos and live feeds played out, depicting the damage and scale of the fires. They didn't look any more serious than usual. Mary contemplated changing the channel.

Then, as she stared at footage of the flames and the firefighters combatting them, an unexpected feeling came over her. Watching the fire burn and these people fight it made her feel tense again, but not in the same way as earlier.

Her heart rate jumped. The next thing she knew, her body seemed to act on its own while her thoughts became paralyzed.

"The fire…" she said in a daze.

Her eyes never diverting from the screen, Mary reached down to her pants with one hand while gripping the wine bottle harder with the other. She didn't consciously undo the button or pull down the zipper. Her hand just seemed to do it without any input from her brain.

Mary moved with urgency, pushing her pants halfway down her thighs. As soon as they were out of the way, she put her hand into her black cotton panties and began feeling around the outer folds of her pussy.

"Mmm…" moaned Mary as a rush of sensations followed.

Her heart rate spiked, so much so she could hear it in her head. Her breathing became deep and ragged, eventually drowning out the newscast. At this point, Mary finally turned away from the TV, more clearly realizing what she was doing. However, she was long past the point of stopping herself.

This was really happening. She was masturbating to the thought of firefighters fighting a raging wildfire. Mary would need to be a licensed therapist to know the implications, but she couldn't bring herself to care. Her body *needed* this, even if her soul might not be able to handle it.

"Yes…the heat!" Mary found herself saying.

She turned her attention back to the TV, which kept showing footage of the fire. She moved her hand with more urgency. She used her thumb to rub her clit, which by now was fully engorged, and used her other fingers to probe her inner folds.

Intense shots of pleasure coursed through her body, causing powerful reactions along the way. Mary's hips jerked and gyrated, as though she were trying to fuck something that wasn't there. The sensations soon intensified, as did her desperation to feel more. She hadn't stopped pleasuring herself since she'd become a sex addict, but she'd never done it like this.

Eventually, the news footage moved on to something else besides the wildfires, but this didn't slow Mary in the slightest. As soon as the news broke into commercial, she closed her eyes and focused her lustful thoughts. The only sounds she heard at this point were her heavy breathing and rapid heartbeat.

In her mind, she wasn't sitting on her couch in her living room after a miserable day. She was standing in a forest, completely naked, surrounded by fire. The heat, the danger and the excitement fueled Mary's lustful actions and the desires that fueled them.

"Hot...so hot...need more!" she said through ragged breaths.

Her body arched more erratically. Basic sensations of pleasure morphed into overwhelming waves of bliss. A ball of the hot, pleasure formed in her core, like a fire that had just been sparked.

Mary could barely feel her hand at that point. She had gone beyond just touching herself. She was *fucking* herself. With her thumb pressing against her clit, she pumped her fingers in and out of her vagina, stimulating the farthest recesses of her sex. The powerful sensations added to the hot feeling in her core. In her mind, the fire grew closer, adding something unique to every sensation.

It didn't make sense. Mary had been sexually aroused by a lot of things, but never anything like *this*. It had many troubling implications. However, she didn't dare rationalize it. She was getting very close to an orgasm the likes of which she hadn't experienced in over a year.

"Ohhh, yes!" she cried out.

By now, her body was so hot that she broke out into a light sweat. Her pants became more mussed while her bra became increasingly uncomfortable.

She released her iron grip on the wine bottle, letting it fall off the couch and onto the floor. Then she used her other hand to push up her bra, freeing her breasts. Her nipples were already fully erect and, without hesitation, she pinched them. It drew her closer to her approaching climax. Like a volcano trying desperately to erupt, she felt the pressure building.

In the burning forest of her mind, the fire had almost reached her. This fire that was the source of the blissful heat was about to consume her body. She couldn't reach out to it herself. She had to make it come to her.

"So close. So...so close..." she panted with growing desperation.

Then, just as she neared the threshold, something strange happened. The imaginary flames began swirling around her naked body — so near, yet just out of reach. Mary watched the fiery imagery of her fantasy take the form of a male figure. Through the smoke, he approached her. There was no more fire, but she still felt the heat radiating from him, guiding her to the ecstasy she craved.

As soon as his face came into view, Mary crossed that threshold from which she could not return. Then, as the orgasmic rush consumed her, she recognized the man and instinctively said his name. "Oh, Peter!" she cried out.

The sound of his name echoed throughout her living room as Mary and her desire converged. Throbbing sensations of white-hot pleasure shot through her like a rocket. The inner muscles of her vagina contracted around her fingers, her lower back arched and she contorted under the force of the powerful feeling. Mary even felt a burst of wetness soak her pussy and her hand. It was by far the messiest, most intense orgasm she had experienced in quite a while.

As waves of pleasure coursed through her body, the mental images of Peter Robert Rogers remained locked in her mind. Every other higher function shut down, making this man her singular focus. It was so intense. Time, place and perspective became blurred. All she could see was her and Peter, surrounded by fire, embracing in heated passion.

The mental image remained with her until the feeling subsided. Her heart rate slowed, her breathing stabilized and her sense of being returned. Then, when Mary finally opened her eyes, the image of her and Peter faded. At that same moment, a cold reality washed over her.

"Damn," she said distantly. "What the hell did I...?"

Mary couldn't finish her own words. There was no getting around it. She *knew* what she'd just done. It completely clashed with the outrage she'd felt only moments ago, but she'd done it anyway.

The first thing she saw was her TV screen. The news was back on and again showed more footage of the wildfires. Then she looked down at herself. Her pants had fallen farther down her legs. Her breasts were exposed, her bra having been pushed aside. However, it was the sight of her hand between her thighs that struck Mary the most.

"Damn," she repeated as more cold reality set in.

Her body finally settled, but not with the typical post-orgasmic afterglow. Mary withdrew her hand from her underwear to assess the scope of what she'd done. It appeared to have been even more intense than she'd first realized.

"Damn," she said a third time.

Looking at her hand and her underwear, Mary realized that her body knew something her mind did not. Her hand was dripping with her juices. Those same juices soaked her underwear, ensuring she wouldn't be able to sleep in them tonight as she had originally planned. She couldn't remember the last time she'd had an orgasm that had been so intense. As good as it'd felt, though, the source of the feeling left her conflicted.

In addition to the mess her body had made, Mary also noticed the wine bottle that now lay on her living room floor. It hadn't been completely empty when she'd dropped it, causing the rest to spill on the carpet. It felt like fate adding insult to injury.

"Great. I made a mess of myself, my clothes *and* my carpet," groaned Mary. "I'm on a hot streak tonight."

Shaking her head in dismay, she got up from the couch and stripped out of her clothing. She also picked up the wine bottle and set it on the coffee table before grabbing the remote to turn off the TV. However, before she did, she got one last glimpse of the footage of the wildfires.

Now standing naked in her living room, Mary Ann Scott tried to process what had just happened. She hadn't come home expecting to pleasure herself to the best orgasm she'd had in a year. She'd left Canicci's Pizza wanting to punch Peter Rogers in the face. Then, in a complete reversal, she'd had a bizarre fantasy of Peter that had led her to unexpected ecstasy. She was no expert, but that couldn't be healthy for a recovering sex addict.

A cold feeling came over Mary as she finally turned off the TV. She hugged her shoulders and dropped her head low, now angry at herself more than Peter. Regardless of how their reunion had turned out, talking to him had really affected her. Whatever that effect entailed, it had made her feel things she didn't understand.

It had evoked emotions that she wasn't ready to process. It frustrated Mary to no end because, like it or not, this man was one of the few friends who'd known her as someone other than a woman whose addiction had come close to destroying her.

Beyond that, there was something else about Peter Robert Rogers that impacted her profoundly. It felt like something that could either help her life or complicate it. Whatever the case, Mary didn't have the energy to deal with it tonight. Shaking her head in defeat, she began cleaning the mess she'd made. The stains on her rug and underwear should be easy. The less obvious mental and emotional messes would probably be much harder.

"Fuck you, Peter. Fuck you for making my life an even *bigger* clusterfuck," Mary said bitterly. "I don't know what you did to me. I should hunt you down and punch you in the dick. But first, I need a cold shower — a *really* cold shower."

Chapter Five

Not long ago, Mary had been the ultimate morning person. She'd once prided herself on getting more work done before sunrise than anyone not working a night shift. She would have woken up early, done yoga, gone jogging, fixed herself a hardy breakfast and been full of energy by the time the sun rose. That kind of dedication had helped make her the successful, passionate, outgoing woman that had captivated everyone around her.

That version of Mary Ann Scott might as well have been from a parallel universe. The effects of her sex addiction, as well as her efforts to treat it, had effectively killed that person. Mary could still wake up early, exercise and do many of the things she'd always done. It just didn't fill her with the same energy it once had. After what had happened the day before, she felt so restless that she didn't expect to captivate *anyone* today.

"Wow. You look like shit, Mary," said Michelle Amber, the front desk manager of Hart World Gym, "and not in the way that hints you had a good time last night."

"Not today, Michelle. For the love of everything good and pure...not today," Mary said, avoiding eye contact from moment she'd walked through the front door.

"Oh, come on, boss. Don't be like that. Whenever you don't let your friends cheer you up, we're all miserable."

"You're not my friends. You're my *employees*. My name is on the deed to this place, last I checked. So please remind everyone of that before they make a scene."

"Will do." Michelle sighed. "Anything else I should warn them about?"

"Not yet, but that's subject to change. If you need me, I'll be in the boxing room punching something."

Michelle wisely kept quiet and let her walk by into the manager's office where she put away her purse and keys. Mary then immediately closed the door to avoid scrutiny from everyone, giving her time to gather herself.

She casually tossed her gym bag aside, turned on her computer then searched through the clutter on her desk until she found her weightlifting gloves. It took her longer than she'd hoped. The office was a far cry from the gym she'd had on South Beach. Even though Mary owned the facility, she still felt like she had taken a step down in life, and it wasn't because this gym catered to soccer moms instead of swimsuit models.

On some levels, she enjoyed working with people who didn't carry themselves like walking centerfolds. There was less ego and they were easier to deal with. However, the confined office reminded her of the difference between an aspiring fitness model and a jaded gym owner in a no-name town.

Mary didn't wait for her computer to finish loading. She didn't answer any voicemails, either. As soon as she found her gloves, which somehow had ended up under a stack of magazines, she put them on and stormed out of her office. Being the face of the gym came with plenty of responsibilities. To carry those out, she had to make Mary Ann Scott less miserable to be around, and that involved some badly needed venting.

"I need to hit something…hard," she said to herself.

This time, Michelle didn't say anything once she'd left her office. Since it was still early, the gym only had a few really dedicated fitness types working out. Mary avoided making eye contact with them, and she hid her face on the off-chance one of them would notice her and push her buttons. She really couldn't afford to be annoyed today. She wouldn't do herself any favors by driving away her customers.

She eventually made it to the boxing room located on the west end of the gym. It had an assortment of punching bags, a regulation boxing ring and sets of specialized weights. The area was closed during this time of day and wouldn't open for another two hours. Hopefully, that gave her the time she needed to get into a better state of mind.

Mary had long since accepted that she would never be the successful, passionate, outgoing woman she once had been. The best she could hope to do was to remain functional enough to run a successful business.

"Just do what Sister Angela told you," Mary told herself. "Don't vent because you want to. Do it because you *need* to."

Without warming up, she began laying into the heavy punching bag in the corner of the arena, hitting with alternating jabs and hooks. Mary had learned early on that venting could help, but only if done properly. Sister Angela had tried to teach her how to do it in a healthy way. She attempted to put those teachings to good use, but on a day like this, she could only be so disciplined.

"I...need...this!" grunted Mary between each punch.

Her heart rate jumped, her breathing grew ragged and her thoughts slowed down. It was not unlike the state she had been in yesterday, minus the bizarre fantasies and overwhelming pleasure. This time, Mary was determined to remain in control. She refused to let her experience with Peter derail her efforts to treat her problems.

Mary soon settled into focus. With every punch, she attacked the many frustrations the past eleven months had wrought. They took many forms, ranging from the people who'd helped enable her addiction to those who'd helped fuel it. Peter Rogers was just the latest, but he was far from the most infuriating.

"Why...do I...keep...punishing...myself...like this?" Mary said, hitting the bag with more fervor.

She barely realized she had said it out loud. It didn't matter. That was why she liked to use this room in private.

That way, nobody could hear her angry musings. She didn't need anyone questioning her sanity any more than she questioned her own.

"That's not an unreasonable question to ask, but I don't think the punching bag is going to answer," said an unexpected voice.

In an instant, Mary was jolted from her focus. Still breathing heavily and flushed with adrenaline, she turned to her right to see the last person she wanted to be there.

"Peter Rogers — and just like that, I feel the urge to punch something else," she said.

"I'm sorry. I wanted to let you continue, but when you started talking to yourself, I got worried."

"How sweet of you," Mary said dryly, "and how the hell did you even find out where I work?"

"It wasn't that hard. There's this thing called the Internet and you are listed as the owner and general manager of this gym."

Mary felt like hitting her head against the wall. She couldn't possibly have been *that* stupid. She hadn't exactly gone into hiding after she'd left Miami. Attaching her name publicly to this gym had made sense from a business standpoint, but it came with personal risks. They had finally come back to bite her.

"I should tell Michelle to do something about that. The last thing I need is people *stalking* me," Mary said, shaking her head in frustration.

"This isn't me stalking you. This is me feeling really bad about what happened last night," Peter said, sounding sincere, yet still keeping his distance.

"You should feel bad...for more reasons than you think."

"I admit it, okay? I'm not sure what you mean about 'more reasons', but I said *all* the wrong things in *all* the wrong ways at the worst possible time. You reached out to me when I needed it. I didn't know just how much I needed it, but I did, and I was a complete dick about it. I pushed you away, accused you of something I shouldn't have and made way more assumptions than anyone should make. I just…"

With every word he said, Peter shifted and squirmed like a kid who'd just gotten caught cheating on a math test. Mary had seen that demeanor before. He did not do well when trying to humble himself. His words finally trailed off, but not before he got his point across.

Then he finally spoke up again. "You know, you could stop me at any time," Peter said.

"You're right. I could," Mary said.

"I'm running low on dignity here, so I'll stop before I go too far. Just believe me when I say that I know I screwed up…bad."

"I believe you. I'm not as vindictive as you remember," Mary said.

"Then let's not throw away our friendship because of one fuck-up. I didn't move back to my hometown to create another reason to hate myself. I came back because I needed to get away from the environment that made me a sex addict."

"I guess we have that in common. We're both back in Hartman County for the same reason."

"Then let's build on it," he reasoned. "Just look at the circumstances here. We both left this place for new lives in flashy new towns, we both got sucked into unhealthy worlds and we both ended up getting our spirits crushed. Seriously, how many other sex addicts find someone they can relate to so well?"

In Mary's experience, arguing over these sorts of things only made existing problems worse. As angry as she was at Peter, she couldn't overlook the situation.

Before her stood a man who'd walked a similar path and suffered a similar hardship. One of the toughest challenges she'd faced when she'd returned to Hartman County was finding others who could relate to her problems. There just weren't that many former fitness models turned sex addicts to talk to, especially in Hartman County. Like it or not, Peter

Rogers could relate. He could understand her struggle.

As Mary contemplated this situation, Peter approached her. She had calmed down to the point where the desire to punch him in the jaw had subsided. He still kept some distance. This time, she couldn't blame him. Considering what she'd done when she'd gotten home last night, it might be best that they not get too close.

"What exactly are you suggesting, Peter?" Mary asked.

"I'm not entirely sure. In fact, I've been trying to figure that out since last night," Peter said. "All I know is this. I don't want the day to end without us coming to some sort of understanding. I'd like it even more if we could help each other."

"I admit I'd like to have someone else to talk to — someone besides a nun or a therapist."

"Then let's try again. My shift at the fire station doesn't begin until eight tonight. What time do you get off work here?"

"I own this place, remember? I get off whenever I'm done working," replied Mary.

Peter laughed. The tension between them eased somewhat. Mary kept smiling, as well — a part of her already willing to take a chance at something that might blow up in her face. It had burned her last night, but being a recovering addict made her adept at taking punishment.

"Still determined to do things your way, eh? Glad to see that part of you hasn't changed," Peter said with a humorous grin.

"My problems haven't *completely* destroyed me. I'm still capable of kicking your ass if you give me a reason to," Mary said.

"Then I'll make sure I don't give you one," he said. "Let's try this… I'll give you my number, and whenever you decide you're done working, give me a call and we'll meet up."

"That sounds way too much like what guys would tell me to get into my panties. Maybe a few extra details would help."

"Good point. Then let's agree to meet some place that's not romantic, intimate or private in the slightest. That way, the temptation is limited and we can focus on the important issues at hand."

"Makes sense." Mary shrugged. "What exactly are these issues, anyway?"

"We can work that out in time. I think the main focus should be *how* we help each other," Peter said. "I don't know how to go about it, but I know I want to give it a try. I just moved back here. I'm still cutting ties with the life I had in LA. If it's okay with you, I'd like to just...talk a little, if that makes sense."

When he put it like that, it made more sense than he'd probably intended. Mary still studied him, searching for any signs of a devious subtext. She saw nothing, nor did she expect to. Peter had never been good at hiding his intentions. This was the same guy who'd once blurted out his plans to cut class in junior high to see a movie. Mary believed his sincerity, more so than she would have if he were anyone else. Even so, she still had reservations.

He had already had a strange effect on her. After one encounter, Mary had gone home and pleasured herself to a news report about a fire after all. Already, his influence on her wasn't healthy. However, a part of her still wanted to connect with him.

In addition, she saw in Peter a desperate man who'd just recently acknowledged his problems. Mary still remembered how that had felt when she'd come to grips with her addiction. She'd had nobody to talk to and nobody to help her. It had been one of the darkest periods of her life.

Nobody should have to go through that alone.

Despite the risks — and the possibility of having to avoid news reports about fires — Mary made her choice. Sister Angela wouldn't approve, but she needed to take a chance. The only alternative was isolation and misery. For any recovering addict, that kind of inaction carried more risk than any other moves.

"Okay. Let's give this a try," Mary said in a more serious tone. "I'll give you my cell number, but I swear to God, if you send me a dick pic—"

"I won't. I promise," Peter said, holding his hands up and giving her an innocent look.

"I mean it, Peter. If at any point you start thinking with the wrong head, I'm wrapping you in cardboard and mailing you back to Los Angeles."

"If that happens, I'll pay the postage," he affirmed.

"Good. Because as much as you pissed me off last night, I want what you want. I want someone I can talk to— someone who won't look at me like I'm an extra in a bad porno."

"That'll be easy for me. I look at you and still see the hard-nosed tomboy who loved showing boys how to kick ass… although you can't expect me to deny that that fiery tomboy has a great rack now," Peter said.

"I wouldn't expect you to," Mary said.

He'd tried to maintain some level of confidence but had only succeeded in part. Mary actually found it refreshing. Even though Peter Rogers had grown into a strong, handsome man, he still had that dorky charm she remembered from their youth. A lot had changed since those innocent years, but having that connection might work to both their advantage.

"But seriously, Peter… I think this is exactly what we need," Mary said. "All the friends and family I have…or used to have… I can't talk to them about this because they don't understand. There are just certain things I can't tell them—painful things that I haven't been able to tell *anyone*."

"Well, you don't have to hold back with me. I'm in the worst possible position to judge," Peter said. "All I know is that I'm a *mess* right now. I need to talk to someone about this stuff. You may or may not think less of me. I may still piss you off."

"I'll keep my temper in check. I promise."

"You don't even have to do that. I just need someone to listen. I might be able to get something like that with the program we're in, but like you said…only you can give me that perspective right now."

Mary remained tense, but neither of them said or did anything to ruin the moment. That alone counted as progress. A part of her still wanted to slap him for what had happened the previous night. Another part of her wanted to hug him for coming to her like this. She managed to resist both. Given their emotional states—and being in a boxing area, for that matter—now wasn't the time to get physical.

Once the tension had settled, Peter gave Mary his number and he left without incident. The frustration that prompted her to take it out on a punching bag had completely faded. Instead, a strange mix of emotions came over her. Two encounters with this man and he had already had some pretty serious effects on her. If the events of last night were any indication, these would likely escalate.

"I may regret this. I may ruin my entire treatment plan," she said to herself. "I'm still gonna risk it. I need to. I just can't wait keep waiting for Sister Angela's methods to work anymore."

Chapter Six

"Okay, class, that's it for today. Hit the showers and rinse the sweat off. You've earned it," Mary said at the conclusion of her final aerobics class.

The announcement often came as a relief to her out-of-shape customers, but this time she shared their sentiment. Her third and final class for the day was over. Her to-do list was officially complete. She'd held a staff meeting with her employees, met with clients who utilized her services as a personal trainer and organized the various exercise classes her gym offered. Checking her phone, Mary confirmed that she had responded to all her emails and voicemails. She had officially run out of distractions.

This day had gone by faster than any Mary had spent that didn't involve heavy drinking. She was usually so focused with her job, pushing her customers and her employees to make this gym as successful as the one she'd had in Miami. Her earlier discussion with Peter ensured that she would remain hopelessly distracted. Even with her thoughts constantly drifting to him, she didn't feel ready for her next encounter with Peter Rogers. Now, she had run out of excuses.

Her class of tired seniors, soccer moms and office dads cleared out of the classroom while Mary packed her things. She kept her phone in her pocket while she put away her weights and sweat bands. She also skipped the part of the class where she singled out customers who had been slacking off. She needed to dedicate her remaining energy to the challenge at hand.

"Is that it? No unmotivational speeches? No telling

everyone they're not pushing themselves?" said Michelle, who helped her clean up.

"Not today," Mary said.

"Should I worry? I've never seen you end a class without busting someone's balls."

"Go home, Michelle. You're done for the day."

"You won't even bust mine? Now I'm *really* worried," said Michelle.

"Don't be," Mary said, rolling her eyes. "Just do yourself a favor and take advantage of my mood. I can't guarantee it'll last."

"Whatever you say, boss. I'll order new punching bags, just in case."

Mary shook her head and zipped up her gym bag. Michelle, being a perky young college student, loved scrutinizing her state of mind. Mary suspected she was fascinated that a former model could ditch such a glamorous life in Miami. She hadn't shared many of the details with Michelle. She — and the rest of her employees, for that matter — just knew that Mary had chosen to leave a toxic environment. That was all they needed to know and all they could possibly understand. For that reason, Mary really needed Peter to be different.

After Michelle and the rest of the customers had cleared out, Mary retrieved her phone and prepared to call Peter. She hesitated, still not ready for whatever their next encounter might bring. However, she hadn't forgotten how much she needed this. She might have to be stronger in ways that no workout could prepare her for.

"Hello, Mary. You're looking more troubled than usual," said a familiar voice.

Jolted from her thoughts, Mary looked up to see Sister Angela standing in the doorway. She was, without a doubt, the last person Mary wanted to see right now.

"Oh, uh...hi, Sister Angela," Mary said awkwardly. "You're—"

"Early? I know. The St. Michael's swim team doesn't meet

for another half-hour. I decided to come early because I wanted to talk to you."

Mary mentally kicked herself. She had been so distracted that she'd forgotten her gym had scheduled a swim meet that evening. As luck would have it, Sister Angela coached the girls' team for the St. Michael's youth athletics league. Knowing she wouldn't approve of her meeting Peter privately, Mary had to be careful with her words.

"Um...sure. What is it?" Mary said, maintaining her composure as best she could.

"Well, I'd like to say it's about why you look so troubled, but I'm afraid we'll have to wait until our next meeting. This is about someone else who just joined the program. I believe you already know him. His name is Peter Rogers."

Her palms grew sweaty. Half the muscles in her body tensed. *Did she find out about my meet-up with Peter last night? Did she sense something had gone wrong?* She was a nun. For all Mary knew, she had some holy power of perception. She tried not to make too many assumptions and pretended to be incredulous at best.

"Yes, um...I do know him," Mary said. "It's been a long time, though, so I may not know him as well as I used to."

"I thought so. You two both grew up here in Hartman County, didn't you?" said Sister Angela.

"Yeah, our dads were old high school buddies. I wouldn't say we were close, but we were friends."

"That's good, because I spoke with him privately before the meeting last night. While I can't talk about what we discussed, I can say that he's in a very vulnerable state... more so than most sex addicts. I'm hoping you could talk to him beyond the brief words I saw you exchange last night."

And just like that, most of Mary's assumptions fell apart. Sister Angela clearly didn't know that she had already spent time with Peter. Mary let out a sigh of relief, but made sure it didn't show. She didn't need to raise any more red flags than she already had.

"Sure. Why not?" Mary said casually. "I mean...we

haven't kept in touch, but I remember him, and I'm sure he still remembers me."

"He does, and quite fondly, I might add. He mentioned you in our conversation as someone who'd had an impact on him," said Sister Angela. "It's his memories of Los Angeles that worry me. The man has a good soul, but that city tainted it. Based on what he told me, he was in the worst possible place for a man addicted to such a vice. The way it utterly destroyed him… My God, Job himself would be impressed."

"What do you mean?" Mary asked, having only partial knowledge of Peter's situation.

"I'm sorry, but it's not my place to say. Peter told me these things in confidence. He said he hated every second we talked about it."

Now, Mary was genuinely curious. Peter hadn't revealed how his problems with sex addiction had destroyed him. He'd only said that he'd indulged in all the vices that Los Angeles had to offer and that reckless indulgence had eventually caught up with him. He must have told Sister Angela a little more, because the older woman seemed very much concerned.

"He was never one for talking about his feelings. How bad was it?" Mary asked.

"*Very* bad…so much so that I said an extra prayer for him last night," said Sister Angela. "He told me about the things he did while in the depths of his addiction. Being a former sinner myself, I admit I was impressed."

"I'm guessing he got a bit too graphic. He tends to do that when he gets upset."

"It wasn't the graphic nature of his sins that concerned me. It was the consequences they wrought. What happened to him… My heavens, words can't do it justice. It hurt him in ways that make me wonder how effective the treatment program will be. I'm concerned he might relapse or abandon CHAOP too soon."

"It…sounds pretty bad," Mary said. "So, what do you

want me to do?"

"While CHAOP usually discourages patients of the opposite sex from interacting, I think this warrants an exception. It's not just because you know Peter personally. His situation is quite similar to yours, and I think the success you've had could help him."

This time, Mary had to be tactful for a different reason. She scoffed at the notion that she had been as successful as Sister Angela had implied. Just because she wasn't having reckless sex with a hot guy every other day didn't mean she was a success. She still felt miserable and empty, but that didn't concern her as much.

She already knew that she and Peter had dealt with similar issues. They'd both moved away from their hometown as teenagers. They'd both built successful lives in major cities that had happened to nourish their addictions. Now, Sister Angela hinted that there were even more similarities. With the looming prospect of meeting up with Peter that evening, her curiosity grew.

"You've done so much good for your soul over the past year, Mary. You should be proud of how far you've come," said Sister Angela.

"Um...thanks," Mary said.

"I mean it. You arrived at my doorstep a 'deviant, unapologetic slut'. Those are your words, by the way, not mine."

"I know. I remember," Mary said.

"Now, look at you," said Sister Angela, gesturing toward her surroundings. "You're a productive member of society. You own a respectable establishment, you've built an admirable career and you've learned to restrain your sinful impulses. By any measure, you are one the Chapman Hill Addiction Outreach Program's success stories."

"I...like to think I am."

"You *are* and I'd like you to guide Peter toward that same success. He made a truly egregious mistake...one I know will haunt him until his dying day. I got a letter from

Gabriel Anderson's family. They are willing to forgive, just as our Lord is willing to. That man doesn't just need to learn restraint. He needs to learn to give forgiveness to himself."

Mary went one step beyond curious. *Who is Gabriel Anderson and why would his family have to forgive Peter?*

With the way Sister Angela had described it, this was serious…way more serious than the struggles of a man who'd slept with one too many married women.

The mention of such a horrible mistake reminded Mary of what had led her to leave Miami. She'd avoided talking about that this, having only told Sister Angela and a few family members. She didn't like thinking about it, either. Sometimes it made her so upset that she wanted to climb to the top of the tallest mountain and scream. However, if someone else had made a similar one, then maybe she could do more.

If Mary had had any hesitation about calling Peter before, it had completely disappeared now. They apparently had way more to discuss than she'd previously thought. If it was as bad as Sister Angela had implied, then he might even end up being more broken than she was, as impossible a notion that seemed.

"I'll see what I can do," Mary said.

"Thank you, Mary," said Sister Angela. "You are a testament to the power of faith and will."

"I appreciate the vote of confidence, but don't use me as a model for success just yet. My recovery is still a work-in-progress, so to speak."

"And I believe you're close to completing the process. I'd like to see Peter be part of that as well. The two of you can be proof that we can overcome our afflictions."

The devout woman added another vote of confidence by giving Mary a hug, as she did with so many others in the program. Mary still questioned her ability to complete 'the process,' as Sister Angela called it, but that was a secondary concern at the moment.

After Sister Angela left, Mary turned her attention back

toward her phone. Without a shred of hesitation, she dialed Peter's number. She just had to be prepared for Peter to affect her in more unexpected ways.

Chapter Seven

"Explain it to me again, Peter. Why is this the best possible place for us to meet?" Mary asked.

"I said we would get together in a place that wasn't romantic, intimate or private. This fits all those qualifications to the letter," Peter said casually.

"It's an amateur softball game."

"At a public park on a hot summer day featuring teams from two different senior centers," he added. "The results speak for themselves."

She had to give Peter credit. It turned out he'd really thought things through. He'd made sure they met in an environment where things wouldn't get heated.

Less than a half-hour after making the call, Mary had met up with him at East Haven Ball Park. The park was nestled between a strip mall and an assisted living facility. It was popular with families and senior citizens, not sexy singles who might tempt a couple of recovering sex addicts. Hartman County didn't have a lot of ball fields, so this one hosted a couple of games a week, and on a hot day like today, the stands were pretty empty.

This allowed Peter and Mary to sit in a remote section of the bleachers just under the scoreboard. Nobody else sat within several rows of them, ensuring they had some measure of privacy. That way, others who'd come by to watch their parents or grandparents play softball wouldn't hear intimate discussions.

In addition, they were out in the open in the late afternoon sun and in plain view of dozens of people to ensure they had enough incentive to restrain themselves. Mary didn't expect that kind of restraint to be necessary, but for a couple of recovering sex addicts, it couldn't hurt to play it safe.

Mary still thought it was a strange place to discuss such serious topics, but she chose not to belabor the point. They'd agreed to meet for a specific purpose. Peter was willing to try again and so long as he didn't screw up like he had last night, Mary was willing to do the same.

"Okay. I'll admit it. This might actually work," Mary said. "Just promise me you won't storm off this time."

"I won't. If I do, I give you legal permission to shoot me in the kneecaps," Peter said.

"I don't own a gun, but I'll figure something out."

"I know you will. I'm trusting you to because—to be brutally honest—I'm tempted to run away. I'm forcing myself to do this...to actually have this conversation with someone. If I'm going to confront my problems, I need to put myself in an uncomfortable situation."

"Am I really making you that uncomfortable?" Mary asked.

"Not in the slightest," he replied. "This is about me confronting my problems, my sins and everything in between."

"And you couldn't do this with Sister Angela?"

"No. I couldn't," Peter said definitively.

"Why not?"

"Because I don't know her like I know you," he said. "You've never been the kind of person who just tells people what they want to hear. And at this point, that's all I seem to be getting from everybody. I need to go farther than that. For the good of my soul—or what's *left* of it—I need someone who isn't afraid to belittle me."

When he put it like that, he made her sound callous and cruel. Even so, Mary believed his every word. Peter carried himself with profound guilt and despair, as though he had been shackled with this burden and couldn't find anyone else to bear it. Mary remembered being in a similar situation when she'd first confronted her addiction, but she didn't remember being so anxious about it.

He remained tense. He stared toward the field where the softball game continued, the two teams of seniors enjoying the late afternoon weather. There was the occasional cheer and the sound of the bat hitting the ball. Peter seemed fixated on these simple noises, as if to distract himself. It could only work to an extent.

Mary was still prepared to run him down if he tried to ditch her like before, but he didn't move this time. She just sat by his side and pretended to watch the game, waiting for him to speak.

"Do you remember the first time you had sex, Mary?" Peter said, finally breaking the silence.

"Not sure if you're trying to change the subject, but… yes," she answered.

"And looking back on it, did you think it would turn into an addiction that would almost destroy your life?"

She took a moment to think about that. It wasn't an outrageous idea, but it was also one that became overly complicated when scrutinized.

"Well, hindsight being what it is, I can't really say. But all things being equal? No, I didn't think it would."

"Then consider yourself lucky. I'm willing to bet your first time was less telling than mine. Ever since I admitted I had a problem, I've thought back to that moment. No matter how I break it down, from the foreplay to the orgasms to the afterglow, there were signs. I saw them clear as day, but I still made the choices that put me on this path."

"Maybe my mind isn't as dirty as I thought, but what kind of choices are you talking about?" Mary asked.

"To answer that, I'll have to give you some of the dirty details. Stop me if it gets a bit too pornographic, but it's the only way I can make my point."

Mary shifted in her seat. She still hadn't forgotten about last night. Just talking to this man in a non-sexual manner got her hormones racing. Now he wanted to discuss the details of his sex addiction. That did not sit well with Mary because it meant testing her and she'd already failed an earlier one. However, Peter had promised that he wouldn't run from this. The least she could do was return the favor.

"I was seventeen years old when I first had sex," Peter began. "That's about two years removed from the day I moved away."

"More like two-and-a-half, but who's counting?" Mary said.

"However long it was, it gave me time to set up shop in LA, hit my growth spurt and go to work making myself stronger. That training you gave me — or whatever you want to call it — really helped. The results were...noticeable, to say the least. And the first girl to notice was this cute, sixteen-year-old bleached blonde California girl named Kimberly."

"Bleached blond? At sixteen? Sounds like a real healthy environment," Mary said dryly.

"It's Los Angeles. Their standards for normal are different, to say the least. I was wholly ignorant of those standards and Kimberly took advantage of that."

"Sounds like she was a bitch-in-training."

"I wouldn't go *that* far, but... Actually, I take that back. That's pretty accurate."

Peter shook his head and rubbed his temples. Mary suspected it hadn't been a simple instance of teenage melodrama, either. It had to be something more serious than that to have put him on this path.

"It didn't help that I've always been an outsider. You know that better than most," he continued.

"I believe the politically correct term is 'dork', but, yeah, I know," Mary said.

"Fair enough, but a big part of that label is seeing how others act through a different lens. I saw Kimberly be like a lot of cute girls, putting themselves out there and trying to connect with the right guy. When they found that guy, it was beautiful. When they didn't? Let's just say it could get downright ugly."

"That's more hopelessly romantic than obscenely pornographic, Peter," Mary said. "Is this really the way you want to talk about your problems?"

"Bear with me, because this is where I start screwing up. You see, I was determined to be the right guy — the one those girls wouldn't regret years later. In a place like LA, there are just too many stories like that. Kimberly was on the fast track to being one of those stories. She had been with this other guy who was a bit too...controlling. So, when she started noticing me — on top of all the other girls who had — I wanted to give her something different. Now that I look back on it, I might have given her too much."

He stopped himself again. Mary kept her silence, focusing on the softball game that was still going on. She had to let Peter tell the story on his own terms.

"Stop me if this sounds like a bad sitcom. A cute girl is frustrated by her ex. She crosses paths with a cute guy who is nothing like him. She gets friendly. She flirts with him. He flirts back, albeit carefully. Then, one afternoon she invites him over to her house. She doesn't admit that her parents are out. It's just sort of implied."

"It does sound like a bad sitcom, but I'm not going to stop you," Mary said.

"Keep in mind that I was still a teenage boy. I was nervous, excited, anxious — everything you would expect from a guy when a cute girl whispers something sexy in his ear," Peter said.

"I'm guessing she said something really raunchy."

"I'd rather not repeat it in its entirety, but at some point she said she wanted to fuck until her legs went numb."

"And I'm guessing that was the first ominous sign?" Mary asked.

"No. That was just foreplay. The signs only became obvious after our clothes came off."

Now it was poised to get detailed. Peter was obviously remaining mindful of the other people in the stands, keeping his voice down so no one could eavesdrop. That meant it must have gotten pretty steamy.

"It started out as fun. I played with her breasts. She fondled my dick. We did the kind of heavy petting you'd expect hormonal teenagers to do when they're hot, horny and unsupervised," Peter said.

"I did all those things at least twice before I turned seventeen. You don't need to list them," Mary said.

"Then, it got serious. I told her I wanted to be inside her. She said she wanted it, too. Somewhere along the way, I said I wanted to be better...to be the kind of guy who went the extra distance."

"You said all this while a cute girl was touching your cock?" Mary said skeptically.

"I...may have used different words, but I got my point across because Kimberly went with it. She had this look in her eye — this look of an animal that had just been let out of its cage."

"Wow. Sounds kinky."

"I'm not sure about that. I didn't know if this was what she wanted or if it was just normal, but I went with it, too. I really did want to be someone better. In this instance, it meant letting a cute girl go to town on me the way she wanted."

He shook his head and scoffed. Mary couldn't tell if he remembered the moment fondly or if it had become tainted over the years. Whatever the case, it was clearly a defining one for him.

"Picture, if you can, a couple of sweaty teenagers in the basement of a suburban house. The guy who'd just recently shed his dorky persona, lying flat on his back while some cute blonde who's nearly a foot shorter pounces on him," Peter said, staring off into the distance. "She smothers her lips all over his face, she rakes her nails down his chest then she rides his dick like her life depends on it."

"Starting to get pornographic, but it's nothing I haven't seen, experienced or triggered before," Mary said.

"Then I'll spare you more details because all the women

told me the same thing. Doing what we were doing — the way we were doing it with them being in charge — felt *really* good."

"That's usually a sign you're doing something right."

"In most cases, it is. I sure thought it was at the time, but keep in mind...I was a teenager. I didn't scrutinize what was happening. I just loved that I was getting laid. Every guy was going to feel that to some extent, but there was something else at work here, something that set the tone for what sex would be like for me."

"What did you do wrong?" Mary asked.

"That's just it. I'm not sure I did anything wrong. I just approached sex the same way I approached my training. I tried to be great and not just good — better and not just competent. In this case, it meant holding out for Kimberly, letting her set the tone so she could get what she couldn't from her ex. I like to think I got the job done as well as any inexperienced teenager. I let her ride me, I fought the urge to come and I waited until she had an orgasm that left my ears ringing for the rest of the day."

"Now you're just bragging," Mary said.

"I think I earned at least *some* bragging rights," retorted Peter. "She said I did set myself apart. She even rewarded me by giving me a blow job and letting me come on her tits. It was incredibly satisfying, but it was just the beginning of a cycle — one that I failed to recognize."

There had been some pride in Peter's voice as he'd recalled his first sexual experience. Mary didn't doubt that he'd exaggerated some details, as most men did. However, she also sensed conflict in his words. As crazy as it seemed, the act of having sex with a cute girl had been secondary. Peter clearly had gotten something else out of it.

It heightened Mary's intrigue, but not just with respect to the details. She recalled her own early sexual experiences. They were varied and extensive, especially during her teenage years. However, Peter's story cast them in a different context.

"Needless to say, I liked what I experienced," Peter said. "I liked it so much that I wanted to do it more, and after Kimberly shared the details with her friends, I had plenty of opportunities. Girls sent me very vivid notes with some very detailed instructions on how to hook up with them. Some of them even included pictures that might not have been legal in some states."

"Sounds like a teenage boy's wet dream," commented Mary.

"It was, but keep in mind...I was still growing at that time. I'd used what I learned from you, working out and getting stronger to avoid being that pudgy dork I was as a kid."

"You're welcome...I guess."

"No need to guess. I'm still grateful, because it came with a lot of benefits. Some of those benefits helped me become a firefighter, and that, I'm proud of. But by the time I hit my senior year, those same benefits had turned me into this big, strong, athletic guy in a town full of sexy, ambitious women. Needless to say, I took full advantage of the situation and that I'm not nearly as proud of—well, not as much as I used to be."

"So...what changed?" Mary asked.

"It's not that something changed, per se," Peter said. "I just realized that what I was doing kept fueling that cycle and I didn't realize how bad it got until it was too late."

He kept coming back to this cycle. He made it sound like a wound that had started small, but had kept growing and growing. It reminded Mary of the burden she'd felt after she'd left Miami. She hadn't realized it had even been a burden until it had finally broken her. Whatever the pain had been, it had done the same to Peter. For someone who'd worked so hard to improve himself, it must have been pretty traumatic.

"How exactly did that cycle play out? Is it as bad as I think?" Mary asked.

"Then some," admitted Peter. "It would go like this. I'd

encounter a pretty girl, go out of my way to tell her I'm better than the men she knows and she'd give me a chance to prove it."

"With sex?"

"Among other things, but yeah. A lot of it came back to sex. In order to be that better man I claimed to be, I had to dedicate myself to art of satisfying women. I pushed myself to be who they wanted me to be, to perform how they wanted me to. I wasn't rich. I didn't drive a Ferrari. But I was a hard-working guy who knew how to get the job done…both in and out of the bedroom."

"You always were pretty motivated. I almost feel bad about pushing it when we were kids," Mary said.

"Don't be. When it came to women, I motivated myself more than anyone," Peter said. "It was a big part of what got the cycle going…especially early on."

Shoving his hands in his pockets, he turned away from the softball game and stared at the ground. He became more emotional, sounding angry with himself. Having had plenty of experience with self-hatred, Mary could understand those feelings.

"Just like my workouts in the gym, I set ambitious goals. Toward the end of high school, I set out to sleep with half the cheerleading squad and most of the girls' soccer team," Peter said.

"And…you succeeded?" Mary asked, not sure if she should be impressed.

"I even slept with someone on the volleyball team for good measure. I'll let you be the judge of that," he said flatly. "Then, after I got involved with the fire academy, I set my sights on every cute sorority girl, aspiring model and waitress in the greater Los Angeles area."

"I'd say that's pretty motivated. Then again, I'd slept with half the basketball team by the end of my senior year, so who am I to judge?"

"Except I went about it in a different way than your typical pussy hound," he continued. "I made it a point to show these women I was better. I did whatever I needed to do to impress them. When they responded, I couldn't jump into bed with them fast enough. I made it my personal duty to seal the deal, so to speak. But once the panties came off, the script got flipped."

"How so?" Mary asked.

She sensed more memories playing out in his mind. Mary knew this because she had seen that look in her own eyes when she'd studied her own reflection. Peter shifted uncomfortably where he sat. Some of the memories must have been too difficult. He seemed to want to keep going, but Mary sensed that they made him feel things he likely had been avoiding for a while.

"I'm still trying to figure out how to describe it without sounding like a bad *Hustler* article," Peter said. "Basically, I willingly got out of the driver's seat and became a passenger. Regardless of whether I seduced a woman or she seduced me, I let the woman set the tone...or *women* in the case of three-ways."

"Don't see how that would make much of a difference," Mary said dryly.

"In any case, I just set aside my strength, my will and my ego, along with my underwear. I let the woman control me, guide me or do whatever it was I needed to do to please them."

"Some women might call that being a considerate lover. Others might call it being a man-whore. I'm sure there are other, less flattering things to call it," Mary said.

"Call it what you want. It worked," Peter said. "I did everything I needed to do to satisfy a woman. Sometimes that meant lying on my back and watching her ride my dick or maybe pinning her up against the wall and humping her brains out. Sometimes it meant bending her over and fucking her ass until she screamed my name. Sometimes it even meant—"

At this point, Mary put her hand up to silence him. Between his details and her weakened capacity for restraint, he was pushing it. She didn't need such specific memories playing out in her head as well.

"Okay, I get it, Peter. You let the woman be in charge. I don't need to know *every* scenario," she said, blushing in ways she didn't usually when talking about sex.

"Sorry about that. I...got carried away," Peter said awkwardly.

"Well, to be fair, I haven't had sex in a while. I'm usually all for perverse chit chat, but..." She let her words trail off so Peter could fill in the blanks. She had to collect herself for a moment. It was a good thing nobody else was watching. They would've seen two grown adults shifting like a couple of kids waiting to get their teeth pulled. It was humbling and awkward in too many ways, but she had no intention of leaving and, it seemed, neither did he.

Eventually, Peter collected himself enough to continue. He gazed back out at the softball field, pretending to watch the game while he recalled this transition from a woman-pleasing stud into a sex addict.

"You're right. I'll skip the part where I tell you how much I enjoyed it. Just assume the things I did for these women got pretty elaborate," Peter said.

"I guess every sex addict feels that way about it early on. I know I did." Mary sighed.

"And I managed to do all this while establishing a career as a firefighter. It turns out being strong and motivated is a great way to get ahead in this field. I went from the guy who checks the tank gauges to the guy organizing rescue operations. I developed a reputation as someone you wanted on your squad when lives are on the line."

"That's a good reputation to have. I'm sure it went even further with the ladies."

"It did. Boy, did it ever," he admitted. "It also accelerated the cycle. I attracted more women, so much so that I didn't have to pursue them anymore. Being a guy with a respectable job in a city where there aren't many respectable people... Let's just say the women just came to me and I ran with it. Then, as time went on, there were…complications."

"In the bedroom?" Mary asked.

"Not really," he answered. "Some of it came from the women. It's easier when you're young and you just want to have fun. You don't want to tie yourself down with commitments and responsibilities. That's why I went out of my way to tell the women I slept with that I wasn't looking for anything exclusive. I wanted to keep things simple, sexy and fun."

"In other words, you just wanted to fuck and not commit."

Peter shook his head and chuckled wryly. "Yeah, that's about right," he said.

"You know, in a lot of places that kind of honesty works against you," Mary said.

"Well, in Los Angeles, it just got me more pussy," Peter said with a shrug. "But even in a place like Los Angeles, people can't be completely callous. Some of these women wanted more than a one-night stand or a quickie. And I'm not going to lie. There were a few times where I wanted more with a woman — something deeper than just great sex."

"So, what stopped you? It couldn't have just been a fear of commitment."

He stopped for a moment. He obviously hadn't given it much thought until recently. That was typical of an addict. Mary had experienced it first-hand, getting to the point where the addiction and the desires no longer fell in line.

"I'm still trying to figure that out," Peter said with a defeated sigh. "I sure as hell didn't think about it at the time. I enjoyed it too damn much, banging all these pretty girls and satisfying them in my own special way."

"It's hard to stop enjoying something as good as sex. As a woman, I guess I should thank you," Mary said.

"Well, I can't say you're welcome, because I ended up breaking a lot of hearts, including my own at times. I'd tell these women that I wasn't ready for a relationship. I'd say I wanted to focus on my career and enjoy my youth."

"Most guys would just lie," Mary said.

"I'm sure I did plenty of that, as well. It didn't matter, because I still hurt those women. But when you're a young, cocky, pretty boy who can easily attract other women, it's easy to shrug off. Then, over time, as you watch your friends and colleagues settle down, it starts to get to you. It doesn't happen all at once, but it still takes a toll."

"So, when did it really start to bother you?"

"Too late to make a difference," answered Peter. "If I ever got upset about it, I just found another pretty girl and drowned my sorrows in her tits."

"That's understandable, I guess, but it *never* works in the long run. Believe me. I know."

"I guess every sex addict knows, to some degree. And in order to learn from it, I guess every sex addict has to find out the hard way. In my case, I don't know how I could've learned any harder."

Peter grew increasingly anxious, rubbing the back of his neck and diverting his gaze in every direction. He looked tempted to run off on her again. He'd already shared plenty of uncomfortable details about his life. This might be too much for him.

In an effort to dissuade him from escaping again, Mary scooted closer. She then reached over and placed her hand on his knee. It was a simple gesture, one that had no sexual connotations whatsoever. It seemed to settle him down, but he remained hesitant.

"How bad was it?" Mary asked intently.

"I'm...not sure you want to know. I'm not even sure I want to tell you," Peter said.

"I think you need to. You've come this far and, unlike sex, pulling out isn't as option."

"That's a bad joke for an issue like this."

"It's not a joke."

Mary offered another gesture, lightly grasping his shoulder and eventually drawing his gaze toward her. Peter might not be ready to do this. It might even do more harm than good, revealing all these details to someone who had yet to figure out her own problems. Even so, Mary remained committed to seeing this through, and she needed Peter to see it through as well.

"I'm not a priest. I'm not your therapist. I'm not your parole officer, either. I'm your *friend*," Mary said. "You know you can tell me anything, right?"

"I know. I just…can't put it in a way that isn't awful," Peter said.

"All the more reason to keep it simple," she argued. "Every addict has that painful moment of clarity. I had mine. And, yes…it was painful. I'm in no position to judge and a perfect position to understand. The way I see it, you won't get this opportunity with anyone else."

He didn't argue her logic. He tried to divert his gaze from her again, but Mary gave his leg a light squeeze to hold his attention. She could literally see him wrestling with it internally, fighting all sorts of conflicting feelings.

Eventually, he gave in. A sense of despair and acceptance was clearly overwhelming him. Taking a deep breath, Peter finally told her.

"Okay, here goes. In the simplest terms, I killed somebody."

Chapter Eight

Her ears were ringing. Mary blinked a few times in disbelief. Peter couldn't have just said what she'd heard him say. It couldn't be that outrageous. *He can't have just admitted to killing someone, can he?*

Her mouth hung open in astonishment. She tried to say something, but no words came out.

Peter let the revelation sink in for a moment, shifting awkwardly under her gaze. He tried to watch the softball game, which was still going on, but this time it offered little distraction for either of them. It wouldn't matter if they were watching a tornado form. It couldn't have shaken Mary from her shocked state.

"So, yeah…it was pretty bad," Peter said, finally breaking the silence.

"What did…? How did…? I, uh… Wow," stammered Mary.

"Need some details?"

"Please," she managed to get out. So many crazy scenarios ran through her mind. *How can something like this make sense?*

It definitely qualified as a moment of clarity, being involved in someone's death. She was sure of that, but Mary still refused to believe it had been as terrible as he'd said.

"It happened three months, two weeks and five days ago. And yes, I have been keeping track. And, yes, I know that's not healthy," Peter said, clearly trying to maintain his composure as best he could.

"I'm…not sure that concept applies here," Mary said, still struggling to remain calm.

"It's a typical Tuesday at the fire station. I was nearing the end of my shift. I was already making plans. I went to the garage to do a final inventory of our gear, as I was required to do. Then, I got this text on my phone. It was from a woman I'd been flirting with — an insanely hot woman who claimed she had every modeling agent in the palm of her hand. She'd once bragged that her pussy brought agents — male *and* female — to their knees."

"She's hot. I get it. How the fuck does this relate to killing someone?" Mary asked.

"Both directly and indirectly," he answered. "In her text, she sent me a picture of her in stiletto heels, black lace panties and nothing else. She also sent an address of the hotel she was staying at, which was only a thirty-minute drive in LA traffic. She told me she would be flying out of town later that evening and this would be our last chance to hook up. I just had to duck out early, get in my car and go to her."

"Still very confused here," Mary said.

"Then here's a crash course on the nature of my job. I'm a firefighter. Lives are on the line when I'm on duty. While we're on our shift, we need to be ready at a moment's notice. If we're not, we put those lives in danger. Being a guy who loves to set high standards, I made it a point to always be ready. Sure, there had been times when I slipped — sometimes because of a woman and other times to catch a movie — but I'd never flat-out abandoned my post. For a woman like this, I didn't think it would be a big deal. Then, as I was running out to my car, I heard the alarm go off."

Mary struggled to see the connection, but these details were clearly important to him. The way Peter described them made them a critical part of this defining moment. He stared off into space, as though he could still hear that alarm ringing in his ear. She resisted the urge to ask more questions.

"I should've responded to that call," Peter said solemnly. "It didn't matter if it was just some idiot teenager who'd lit a trashcan on fire. It was still an emergency and I was the guy my crew relied on to go the extra mile. I was a leader and an example to everyone."

"*Was?*" Mary asked.

"I know what I said," he replied, "because the moment I decided to meet up with a beautiful woman instead of doing my job, I threw away that title. I knew it was wrong. I even hesitated, giving myself plenty of time to change that decision, but...I didn't."

Now dropping his head low in shame, Peter swallowed a couple of times in another clear sign of emotional strain. Reliving the moment was obviously traumatic. It didn't explain how that related to killing someone, but it revealed a profound upheaval in his life.

As the shock wore off, Mary continued to listen. She gave Peter the time he needed. The strong man he'd grown into seemed to revert to the insecure boy she'd known in her youth. Just as she had in years past, Mary tried to give him strength.

"Maybe you should stop. Maybe this is something I don't need to know," Mary said.

"No. I want... No, I *need* to tell you," Peter said, his strength returning. "What happened next is kind of a blur. I turned off my phone, ran to my car and drove off. I still remember the sound of the siren. I even remember hearing the fire truck pull out. After that, I shut everything out. My dick was in the driver's seat. I didn't allow myself to think any other thoughts."

"That woman better have been worth it," Mary said.

Peter scoffed and shook his head in dismay. "*That's* the pathetic part. I don't even remember it being that special. I met her in her hotel room. We had a few drinks, then we ripped our clothes off and fucked. It really wasn't any different from the dozens of other pretty girls I'd slept with. She just had a slightly nicer rack than most of them."

"So...it wasn't the mind-blowing sex she promised you?"

"Not really. It was just sex. We got into bed, we talked dirty and we humped each other's brains out. I did what I always did. I'd long since stopped overthinking it, just lost myself in the pleasure. Hell, I don't even remember going home that night. It wasn't until morning that I realized how badly I'd screwed up."

The strain in his voice escalated. He made an angry fist and cursed himself under his breath. It probably wasn't the first time, either. Mary had done more than her share of self-loathing, but not like this. She was tempted to give him some space but stayed close. If he really needed to tell her, then she needed to be there to listen.

"As soon as I turned my phone back on, I saw a long string of missed calls and voicemails," Peter continued. "Derek Sanchez, one of the lieutenants, had sent most of them. That call I ignored wasn't just some stoner who'd fallen asleep on his couch. It was this old apartment complex in West Hollywood. Some rats got into a bundle of outdated fuse boxes, chewed through some wires and ignited the wooden infrastructure. Most of the people on the lower levels got out, but…there was this family on the top floor. They were throwing a big family party to celebrate this guy's eightieth birthday. He was in a wheelchair, so when smoke started filling the building, they were reluctant to leave."

"Understandable," Mary said, "but don't all firefighters train for that sort of thing?"

"Of course we do, but training only goes so far when you don't have the right equipment. Remember how I said I was checking the gear before I got that call? Well…" He cursed himself again, giving himself the brunt of the blame for what happened. Mary could only assume it was worse than anything he could describe.

"My squad—the squad I was responsible for—didn't have enough oxygen in their tanks," Peter said solemnly. "It was *my* job to make sure those tanks were full. It was *my* job and I neglected it…all for some meaningless sex with some bimbo I haven't seen since."

"You can't blame yourself entirely," Mary said.

"It gets worse. Even without full oxygen tanks, they still

could've saved those people. I could've led them. Hell, I had led them through way worse situations before. Even on my worst day, this wouldn't have been a problem. Except…I wasn't there. I *should've* been there, but…I wasn't."

Saying those words out loud clearly hurt. Peter eventually stopped cursing himself and slumped down on the bench in defeat. Mary knew that feeling, as well.

"To their credit, my squad made a hell of an effort. However, they only ended up making things worse," Peter said solemnly. "They broke down a few too many walls, causing parts of the roof to collapse. Some got injured, which slowed them down even more. This made the situation even more dangerous for the family. The smoke kept getting thicker. The flames kept getting hotter. By the time someone made it through…"

Peter had to stop again. Tears had formed in his eyes — something Mary had never seen before. Growing up, he had been so reserved. It had taken a lot to get him to show much emotion. After reliving the painful moment, he looked ready to break down.

In an effort to console him, Mary gave his hand a firm squeeze. It seemed to help somewhat, but he was still very tense, breathing steadily and swallowing hard to contain his emotions. This time, she didn't ask him to stop. She could've filled in the blanks from here, but Peter needed to finish sharing his tormented recollection.

"Nine people were in that room — three men, four women and two children," Peter said, the memories still painfully vivid. "They all died — every one of them. By the time my squad got to them, the smoke had killed them. The news called it a tragedy. My squad called it a botched rescue. I call it what it is…a crime."

"Peter, you can't—" began Mary, only to be cut off.

"Yes, Mary, I *can*," Peter said angrily. "It was criminal negligence on my part. I wasn't there. I didn't do my job. I was so fucking mad at myself. Anything in my condo that wasn't nailed down, I *threw* it. If it was nailed down, I punched it. Every beautiful woman I'd ever slept with… It now felt so…so tainted."

Mary opened her mouth to say something, but no words came out. There was nothing she could say to undo the impact of what had happened. She could only try to understand it within the context of her own pain. However, he still wasn't finished.

"I was ready to throw myself onto the steps of the nearest police station," continued Peter, still brimming with anger. "I prepared a confession. I even prepared hand-written letters to every relative of that family. Luckily – or unluckily, depending on how you look at it – the station chief stopped me. I told him everything. I told him about the woman. I told him how I left my shift early. I even laid out in perfect detail how I could've saved those people if I had been there. I *wanted* to pay for my crimes."

"But he didn't see it that way, did he?" Mary surmised.

"No. He couldn't have," Peter said. "We did end up getting sued by the owner of the building. I was ready to accept full responsibility, but the case got dismissed as soon as the insurance companies stepped in. By the letter of the law, the only thing I was guilty of was ducking out of work. The worst that would have gotten me was a suspension, a pay cut and a reprimand. I would've accepted all of that and more, but all the chief did was reprimand me. He didn't even demote me or dock my pay. He said my record was too good to be tainted by this tragedy."

"Except it still wasn't just a tragedy in your eyes."

"Don't talk like you understand, Mary," he said in a harsher tone. "I did something I *knew* was wrong, but I didn't care. Nine people died…all because I couldn't turn down a chance to fuck some nameless bimbo. Now, I have to live with that until the day I die. And honestly, I don't know if I can."

The full weight of Peter Rogers' burden finally became clear. In his mind, *he'd* killed those people. It didn't matter what the law had said. It didn't matter what his colleagues had said. He blamed himself for those deaths. There weren't too many people who could understand that kind of burden. However, Mary was one of those select few.

A heavy silence fell over them. The sounds of the softball game kept it from getting too awkward. Even in the hot summer wind, a cold feeling came over her. Mary kept her hand on Peter's, offering what comfort she could. He remained distraught, obviously reliving the impact of that decision. Mary gave him time to deal with that while doing what she could to support him.

The shock she'd felt earlier had morphed into something completely different. The events of the previous night took on a very different meaning, as did her own personal burdens, but just understanding Peter's plight wasn't enough. Hearing his story put her problems in a new context. Now, the dorky boy turned handsome man sitting next to her had become someone else entirely.

"Gabriel Anderson," Mary said, finally breaking the silence.

"What?" Peter said, tensing at the sound of the name.

"Gabriel Anderson," she repeated. "*That's* the name of the man whose family died in that fire, isn't it? He was the man they were celebrating that day."

"How did...?"

"Sister Angela mentioned that name," Mary said before he could finish. "She also said the family sent you letters saying they forgave you."

Peter groaned something under his breath. He was cursing Sister Angela for telling her, but she sensed that he still directed the bulk of the anger at himself.

"Does it really matter?" he questioned.

"Yeah, I think it does. I think it matters a *lot*," Mary said.

"Well, their forgiveness doesn't matter to me. Why the hell would Sister Angela tell you about that? Don't nuns take a vow of secrecy or something?"

"You're thinking about doctors and priests. And even if there was an oath like that, I don't think Sister Angela would keep it. She'll bend the rules if she thinks it'll help people cope...although her preferred method of coping is still suspect."

"That still doesn't explain why she told you," Peter said.

"It's not for the reason you think. She came to me earlier today, saying she was worried about you. She asked me to reach out to you. She told me this because she thought I would understand your problems better than anyone else. Now I know she was right."

Peter looked at her strangely, clearly neither believing Sister Angela's reason for telling her nor accepting that she was right. However, Mary was already convinced. It was tragic, but promising in some ways, because it meant he might be able to understand her pain in the same way she understood his.

She kept trying to comfort him. She even tried to flash that goofy smile that had always seemed to work on him when they had been kids. This time, however, it didn't.

"I...I can't do this anymore," Peter said in a distressed tone.

He abruptly pulled his hand out of her grip then stood. Mary did, as well, and she tried to reach out to him again, but he pulled back and began walking away. Unlike last night, though, Mary didn't get angry.

"Peter, wait!" she called out.

"I've had enough of this today, Mary," Peter said. "Thanks for listening, but I think I'm worn out."

He started walking faster, navigating the stands like an obstacle course to get to the exit. Mary did her best to keep up with him. She could tell he was still upset, hiding his expression and avoiding awkward gazes from everyone he passed. She couldn't let him run off this time. She might end up losing more than just a friend.

After making it out of the stands and halfway toward the parking lot, she managed to catch up. He tried cutting across the lawn of the park, but Mary kept pursuing him. When she finally caught up, she grabbed his shoulder to stop him.

"Peter, come on. Don't do this," Mary urged him.

"Damn it, Mary. What do you want from me?" barked Peter.

He turned around and shoved her arm away. He tried to send her back with his upset glare, but Mary refused to be scared off.

"I want you to listen for a moment. I also want you to try something, because I really think I can help," Mary said, staying calm yet assertive.

"I don't know what kind of help you can offer, but I'm pretty sure I don't need it right now," Peter said.

"Come on, Peter. Your eight-year-old self was more convincing than that and he couldn't lie about stealing my Halloween candy."

"We're not kids anymore. Don't talk down to me like I'm the puny little shit I used to be."

"I know you're not that same boy. You're a man now — a man who has been stumbling around the dark, tripping over his own ass trying to deal with his problems. You know you can't do this alone. You've indirectly admitted it."

"How do you figure that?" he scoffed.

"Because if you really believe what you just said, you wouldn't have told me everything in the first place," replied Mary. "Look me in the eye and tell me I'm wrong."

His lips quivered. He *had* to know she was right. He wouldn't admit it overtly. Peter had always hated admitting he was wrong. He didn't have to in this instance. His silence gave Mary the answer she needed.

She gave him a moment to calm down, letting him fume so the emotions could run their course. Now they stood alone in the middle of a clearing in the late afternoon sun. They had no distractions from the softball game. They didn't have to worry about being careful, either.

They had officially put themselves in the exact situation they'd promised to avoid, but Mary was willing to take that chance. She had taken so few over the past months, but now she had an opportunity to do something bold.

"What the hell are we doing here, Mary? What are we supposed to gain from this?" Peter asked, now more exhausted than angry.

"I'm still trying to figure that out. After what you just told me, I have a somewhat different perspective on my problems," she said, "but I have an idea on how we can help each other. Not saying it's a great idea, but I'm willing to try it. Are you?"

"That depends. What is it, and how crazy is it?"

He still looked very skeptical. Mary shared some of that. She had since turned off the part of her brain that urged her to second-guess herself. She had been doing that since she'd admitted she was a sex addict. In hearing Peter's story and relating it to hers, she saw a few common themes.

Looking at her friend, Mary concluded that Peter didn't have eleven months to deal with this problem through the program. Even if he did, he didn't deserve to feel the misery and emptiness that she had experienced over those months. When she moved back to Hartman County, she'd had nobody to help her through the personal turmoil. Peter didn't have to go through that...nor should he.

With this in mind, Mary turned her idea into action. She took a step closer to Peter, much closer than she had dared thus far. If Sister Angela were present, she would've pushed them apart out of fear that this could trigger too much temptation. However, they needed to tempt each other...albeit in a wholly unique way.

"Hug me," Mary said.

"Uh...come again?" Peter asked.

"Hug me," she repeated. "Don't ask for permission. Don't wait for me to make the first move. Just *hug* me."

"But—"

Mary put her hand up to silence him. She'd had a feeling he would react that way. She needed him to stop overthinking the situation, having done way too much of that herself.

"Before you overanalyze, let me point out something. From what you've told me, you don't just take what you need. You often wait for someone to guide you to it. Maybe you needed that as a kid, but as an adult it's different," explained Mary.

"I'm not sure where you're going with this, but continue," Peter said.

"You went out of your way to give others what they need. Sometimes it involves saving them from burning buildings, sometimes it involves giving them great sex. But what about *your* needs? If you don't fulfill them, then it's going to mess you up. That's a given."

"Are you speaking from experience or just plain common sense?"

"A little of both, actually," admitted Mary. "When you're an addict, common sense isn't so common, so why not give it a try? You need to connect with someone in a way that doesn't involve swapping body fluids. Well, here I am. I'm not going to give you permission. I'm just going to give you a chance to do it. The choice is yours, and for once, I'm going to trust a handsome, attractive man to make the right one."

He gave her another confused look. He didn't ask any additional questions, either. That was a good thing, because Mary doubted she could explain it more if she tried. She was operating on a whim, hoping something would come of it.

Another silence followed. Mary could tell that Peter was both conflicted and skeptical. She could hardly blame him. This sounded so strange on paper, but seemed so necessary in practice. She was doing something that Sister Angela had told her to avoid, putting them in situations where the temptation might be too great. She sought intimacy during a time when she felt vulnerable, but she was willing to risk it with Peter Rogers.

"Peter, I..." began Mary in another effort to break the silence.

But before she could get another word out, Peter made his choice. Acting on a whim, just as Mary had done earlier, he threw his arms around her and embraced her. It caught her off-guard, but she accepted it nonetheless.

Silence once again followed, but it wasn't least bit awkward. Instead, Mary felt a powerful warmth within his embrace. It felt intimate but not overtly sexual. It was not foreplay or flirting. This was something totally different.

"Thank you, Mary. Thank you…for what you've done for me," Peter said, his voice once again strained by emotions.

"You're…you're welcome, Peter," Mary said.

This time, he conveyed positive sentiment. Peter clung to her like a warm blanket on a cold winter night, which was oddly fitting under the hot summer heat. Mary smiled at the feeling and hugged back, wrapping her arms around his waist and resting her head against his broad chest.

He was breathing heavily and she could feel the rhythm of his heartbeat. Despite his well-toned muscles, his arms actually trembled. This strong man had become weak in her arms. It was profound in so many ways—more so than she'd ever expected.

"Thanks for not running this time," she found herself saying.

"I'm glad you didn't let me," replied Peter.

The shift in his voice revealed he was smiling. It assured Mary that her crazy idea had worked. It had been simple. It didn't solve all their problems, but it was a welcome change from the isolation and frustration they had endured.

However, the more they lingered in the embrace, the more they tempted themselves. At some point, Mary's body remembered that a handsome man had his arms around her. That triggered some responses that she didn't wish to happen. The fiery heat she'd felt the previous night emerged again, making her legs weak and her inner thighs moist. She tempered her body's response as best she could, but it still tested her restraint.

Easy girl, she told herself. *Not here. Not now.*

Before it got too heated, she ended the embrace so they could each catch their breath. His hands remained on her shoulders, the tension having faded considerably. He was still smiling. Mary smiled back, hiding whatever arousal she may have felt from his touch. She had no idea where things would go from here, and for once, she didn't mind.

"I want to keep doing this," Peter said, as though he'd just had an epiphany.

"You want to keep hugging? That may get a little weird," Mary said in a humorous tone.

"No. I mean *this*," he said, gesturing to the two of them. "You're right. I need this. I can't confront this problem alone. Just moving back here—removing myself from my problems—isn't enough. I need something...no, *someone* who can be an anchor."

"And you want me to be that anchor?" Mary asked.

"Why not? You know me so well. Hell, you know me better than anyone ever has or has even tried to. We were a part of each other's lives before sex entered the picture. And since we happen to be dealing with the same problem, why not help one another?"

"You make it sound so logical. It almost makes too much sense."

"Maybe that's a sign. Then again, you've been dealing with this longer than I have. Just answer me this. Is what you were doing before working any better? You didn't give the impression it was."

Mary wanted to scold him for being so observant. That didn't make him any less right. He'd followed the same twisted logic she had when she'd told him to hug her. It was still risky, the two of them interacting at a time when their addictions still affected them. However, they had just gotten a taste of those rewards. While it had tested her restraint, it had left Mary wanting more of the feeling.

"I'm...going to plead the fifth on that, but assume I'm open to a new approach," Mary said.

"Sure. I can make those kinds of assumptions," Peter said

with a half-grin.

"Don't make too many, pretty boy," she retorted. "Now, tell me how this is going to work. How exactly are we going to help each other?"

He let go of her shoulders and contemplated this for a moment. Mary doubted he understood what he was suggesting, but the self-loathing she'd seen earlier had faded. She now saw a man who was ready to take more chances, even at a time when he was so vulnerable. Mary still couldn't help but be intrigued.

"I still want to stay in the Chapman Hill Addiction Outreach Program. I don't think either of us should ditch that just yet," he began.

"Yeah. Probably a good idea," Mary said.

"But outside that program, I think we should have our own meetings — meetings that are out in the open, in a public place and in a non-romantic setting. This way, we can share the things we're not ready to share with others. I'm not going to lie to you. I am *not* ready to tell Sister Angela all the details I just told you."

"I don't blame you. Neither would she, for that matter."

"But I feel like I can talk to you. I feel like I can be around you and not have it go the wrong way," Peter said.

He still described it as though it were so logical. Mary saw the appeal, having someone outside work and CHAOP she could connect with. However, there were still risks and they weren't easy to overlook.

"How can you be so sure it's not going to go wrong?" Mary asked. "One minute we could be watching a softball game, the next we could be fucking each other senseless under the bleachers. Not to make that sound unpleasant, but I'm trying hard not to relapse here."

"It won't happen, because we're both recovering sex addicts. You know where I'm coming from. You know what I want out of this. And as it just so happens, I'm in a unique position to help you, also."

"I don't disagree. Even if it makes sense, it's still

something that bends the rules of the program," Mary said. "Sister Angela makes a big deal about avoiding temptation, especially for newbies who also happen to be attractive men."

"I get that, but you and I weren't afraid to bend the rules as kids, and it paid off any number of times," Peter said, flexing his muscles to prove his point.

"That's different. We were kids, remember?"

"Now you're just trying to talk yourself out of this, and not for the right reasons."

"I'm not trying to—" she began. She realized she was overthinking the situation. She was doing exactly what she'd told herself *not* to do. She ended up biting her lip, letting herself look foolish.

"Just look at the basics here, Mary," he said. "You want to get better. I do, too. The incentives are there. The history is there. The comfort is there. So, let's be *responsible* sex addicts and face the cold, hard facts. We can't get through this alone without tormenting ourselves. So why not try something a little bolder?"

He sounded downright excited about this, a major shift from his previous state. Peter looked at Mary as if she were the key to dealing with his problems. That put her in a difficult position, but one that presented a unique opportunity.

She didn't bother debating him. Even if she wanted to, she would fail. Peter had that glint in his eyes that Mary had never turned away from when they were kids. As an adult who had endured months of misery and self-loathing, it was even harder to avoid.

He was right on too many levels. They needed each other and she needed a better way to confront her addiction. Sister Angela's approach just wasn't cutting it. Knowing all the risks and potential problems that might arise, Mary smiled at her childhood friend and pulled him into another embrace. It wasn't as deep as the one before, but it got her point across.

"Okay, Peter. Let's try…whatever the hell you want to call this," Mary said.

"Great! I promise you I'll approach this the same way I approached your training back in the day," Peter said, now brimming with energy.

"You don't need to promise me *anything*, Peter. We're a couple of recovering sex addicts trying to rebuild our lives. Right now, let's take things one day at a time."

"I understand. Believe me, Mary, the last thing I want to do is complicate our lives more than they already are."

Chapter Nine

"Mmm...so hot. Need more!"

It was happening again. A powerful heat formed within Mary's core. Like the smallest of sparks growing into a raging inferno, it drew her into a state of intense desire. She needed this heat to consume her. She needed to feel the burn through every nerve in her body.

Mary's brain once again ceded control to other parts of her body — namely, the parts between her legs now driving her actions. Her pussy burned with arousal. The outer folds of her vagina were fully engorged. She followed this need with more vigorous teasing.

She was pumping her fingers in and out of her vagina while she rubbed her clit with her thumb. The other hand was pressed against the wall, allowing Mary to support herself as her legs became weak under the heat. In this dazed state, she vigorously pleasured herself in a reckless pursuit of another orgasm.

She could barely recall how she'd ended up like this. Mary remembered getting home from work, unpacking some groceries then stripping out of her sweaty workout clothes to take a shower. After that, everything got a little fuzzy. Mary didn't know what had led her this heated round of self-pleasuring, but she knew who to blame.

"Peter..." she said with a desperate gasp.

Everything around her felt so hot, but it had nothing to do with the fact that her shower was still running. Just saying his name made Mary's heart race, giving her the energy and motivation she needed to push herself to the brink of orgasm. With soap still dripping from her breasts and parts of her hair, she was ready to climax.

As the inferno consumed her, Mary leaned back against the wall. This allowed her to fondle her breast with her free hand. She squeezed and pinched her nipple while pumping her fingers into her pussy.

"Oh, Peter!" Mary cried out.

As soon as she said his name, the fire within turned into a hot surge of pleasure that shot up through her body like a rocket. The inner muscles of her vagina spasmed, her thighs tensed and her knees buckled. With her back against the wall, Mary ended up sliding down to the floor, her body throbbing with orgasmic bliss. As her moans echoed throughout her shower, she kept shouting Peter's name.

Mary said it like a reflex. It had somehow become deeply connected to her most basic desires. It complicated something that should've been simple. Even a recovering sex addict needed a good release every now and then. But this didn't feel so basic anymore.

"Damn...I did it again," Mary said distantly.

She opened her eyes to confirm what she already knew. Sitting on the wet floor, her hand buried between her thighs, Mary saw yet another case in which Peter Rogers had affected her. Most of his effects on her had been good, but there were still some lingering issues, and this was one of them.

Mary took a moment to steady her breathing, letting the orgasmic sensations in her body pass. Then she removed her hand from between her thighs, which now dripped with her juices, and washed it under the pouring water. Once the strength returned to her legs, she rose and rinsed off. She even adjusted the faucets to make the water a little colder in an effort to temper any lingering desires, even though it was too late to wash off the emotional aftereffects.

Once finished, she turned off the shower and grabbed a towel. As she dried herself, she let out a defeated groan. This hadn't been the first time this had happened—her pleasuring herself to thoughts of Peter Rogers—but it was becoming uncomfortably regular.

"Why do you keep doing this to yourself? Do you *want* to make things harder?" Mary asked herself.

Shaking her head in dismay, Mary wrapped the towel around her naked body and stepped out of the shower. She wiped away the fog that had built up on her mirror and gazed at her reflection. She looked pretty anxious for a woman who'd just had an orgasm. She might have been overwhelmed if this had been an anomaly. However, a lot had changed since she'd reconnected with Peter and that didn't just apply to her masturbation habits.

"Two weeks," Mary said to her reflection. "It's been a little over two weeks since you and Peter agreed to help each other. And for all the good he's done, you *still* can't help yourself."

Two weeks ago, that would've been a lot easier. Her inability to berate herself was another testament to Peter's effect on her. It still didn't stop her from trying.

"A few dirty thoughts is one thing, but this is more than a few," Mary continued. "It's healthy for a young woman to masturbate, but you're pushing it. How many times is this now? Once a day? Twice? You're just lucky you had the decency to do it in the shower. Last week, you got yourself off while stuck in traffic. What does *that* say about you?"

She already knew the answers to those questions and some of them didn't sit well. Others were a bit trickier, going beyond Peter Rogers and the various problems associated with recovering sex addicts.

"Cut the crap. You *know* what it says. Eleven-and-a-half months, plus the time you spent with Peter, and you still feel so...incomplete. Peter helped fill the emptiness, but there's still something missing — something you won't allow yourself to think about. Pretty soon, you'll have taken all the steps you promised to take after you left Miami. And if, after all that, you're still crippled by your addiction... then what?"

That question confounded her more than anything she

did to get herself off. In just a few days, she'd have to stand up in front of everyone at the Chapman Hill Addiction Outreach Program and say she had stuck with the program for a full year. Everyone, especially Sister Angela, expected her to be glowing with renewed spirit. They expected her to say that she had conquered her addiction, having cured herself of the ills of her unhealthy desires.

Even before Peter had come back into her life, she'd doubted she could meet those expectations. Now, after trying to deal with her addiction in a new way, those doubts had only escalated.

"You're either misguided, stressed or crazy," Mary said. "Either way, you'll need to figure it out. If your brain doesn't do its job, then you can expect other parts of your body to take over."

Having belittled herself enough, Mary sighed and finished drying herself. She grabbed another towel to dry her hair. Then she used a blow-dryer and brush to fix it up. Once finished, she removed her towel, retrieved her bathrobe and exited her bathroom.

She had another CHAOP meeting that evening, so she had to make herself presentable at some point. She also had another get-together with Peter afterward. After what she'd just done in the shower, there were bound to be complications for both of them. She had gotten pretty good at coping, but at some point, she had to do more than just that.

As Mary contemplated how to deal with all these issues, a brochure for the Chapman Hill Addiction Outreach Program caught her gaze. She kept it on the night stand next to her bed, as suggested by Sister Angela, to remind herself of her goals. It contained details about the program, as well as a few tips for those recovering specifically from sex addiction. Mary had read it over multiple times. She found herself opening it up anyway and turning to a specific section.

"Understanding sexual addiction. Accepting the damage

and overcoming its grip," she read aloud. "Sex addiction is one of the more complex addictions we deal with. It sets itself apart from substance abuse by corrupting a natural, beautiful act. Those afflicted engage in deviant sexual behaviors that obscure and undermine their personal and spiritual well-being. With our personal, comprehensive and time-tested approach, we help sex addicts understand the harmful nature of these behaviors and overcome these destructive urges."

Mary had read this text dozens of times before. She always heard Sister Angela's voice when she read it, not her own. She never doubted the older woman's commitment. The nun sincerely believed that she could help everybody overcome these 'destructive urges,' as she called them.

She wasn't like most nuns. She'd avoided getting overly religious, never becoming too preachy with anyone or saying they also needed to adopt the mentality of a nun. At the same time, her piety often made her difficult to relate to, in spite of her past. She claimed she understood, but that understanding was limited.

She found herself re-reading the last sentence a few times. The idea of understanding her behaviors and overcoming the urges had made sense when Mary had first entered the program. After re-connecting with Peter, though, she wasn't so sure anymore.

"I'm *way* behind the curve when it comes to urges. That's for damn sure," Mary said. "Understanding the nature? I guess I'm not so sure where I stand there."

She continued flipping through the brochure, reading over all the tips and tricks she had learned over the past year. They ranged from saying certain prayers to keeping a journal. Mary had tried some of those methods. Some had helped, but none had made her feel like she had truly dealt with her problem.

"Maybe I need a new approach," Mary said. "What I did before wasn't working. What I'm doing now with Peter? I *guess* it's working, but I'm not sure I understand it."

With parts of her body still tingling from her orgasm, Mary set the brochure aside and got dressed. She had a new goal for tonight's meeting. She needed to discuss this with Sister Angela and Peter. Taking things one day at a time was no longer an option. She needed to get more proactive.

Mary threw on some underwear, a pair of jeans and a red T-shirt. She still had an hour or so before she had to leave for the meeting. That gave her time to pay a few bills and take care of some menial tasks, ensuring she could focus all her effort on the challenge at hand.

She was about to get going when she heard her cell phone go off. Assuming it was someone from work, she checked the caller ID. To Mary's surprise, the number belonged to Sister Angela.

"This *can't* be a good sign," she said with dread.

She contemplated letting it go to voicemail. She purged that thought from her mind and answered it, as anyone in the Chapman Hill Addiction Outreach Program was expected to do.

"Hello?" Mary said anxiously.

"Mary, I'm sorry to call you like this, but we have a situation. I need to speak with you at the community center as soon as possible." said Sister Angela in an urgent voice.

"Why? What's going on? And why call me?"

"I...I can't say it over the phone. Someone called me, and...it's just too awful. Please just...just get over here! You need to see it for yourself."

Chapter Ten

"Wow. I'm not impressed by much—being a recovering sex addict and all—but seriously... Wow!" Mary said in utter astonishment.

"I know. It's terrible, isn't it?" lamented Sister Angela.

"That's not the only word I would use to describe this, but, in this context? Yeah, I'd say it's pretty bad."

A recovering sex addict could expect to encounter many problems over the course of their treatment. Mary had certainly endured more than her share, but she'd never run across anything like this. While Sister Angela anxiously paced around the empty meeting room at the community center, Mary watched the problem play out before her on a laptop computer screen.

Susan Michaels, the same woman who had claimed to be a beacon of renewed chastity a couple of weeks before, had fallen back to rock bottom in a very graphic way. In a video that had been uploaded to the Internet less than six hours ago, this middle-aged woman was engaging in some extraordinary acts of sexual excess that included bondage, submission and gangbangs.

Even by Mary's standards, it was pretty extreme. Susan had exchanged the overly conservative attire she'd often worn to meetings for the garb of a full-blown Dominatrix. This included thigh-high boots, a corset that exposed her breasts, a spiked collar and crotchless panties. Even at her most depraved, Mary had never worn something that bold. However, the attire didn't shock her nearly as much as how Susan used it.

On the video, which Mary had watched twice already,

Susan had some masked man bound by handcuffs and pinned the floor. She had her heel on his neck while firmly tugging on a chain connected to his collar. It caused the man discomfort, but he appeared to enjoy it in a perverse sort of way. As she dominated him completely, she used a leather-studded whip to spank him repeatedly on his partially exposed ass.

"That's right! Take it! Take it like a good slave!" spat Susan, her voice the complete antithesis of the mild-mannered woman Mary knew.

It only got worse from there. After she'd finished whipping the man, two more had entered the area, which had been decorated like a medieval dungeon. They each wore the same leather masks as the man she'd whipped. Together, they orally pleasured her. One sucked on her nipples. The other flicked his tongue in and out of her vagina. This further emboldened Susan and she struck the man under her even harder.

"Yes! Don't you *dare* stop." she said menacingly. "You *will* pleasure me. You *will* give me what I want. If you don't, I'll just have to punish you even more."

Even Mary couldn't help but blush. She kept on watching until Susan forced the man going down on her to lie on his back so she could fuck him. He did so with the utmost obedience, letting Susan ride him with a dominating fervor that seemed unfit for a woman of her stature. If her loud moans were any indication, she had kept this pent up for quite some time. She made noises that Mary had never heard before during sex. Even after watching it more than once, Mary still couldn't believe it.

The idea that the same woman Mary had envied a few weeks before would do something like this was shocking enough. The idea that she'd live-streamed it over the Internet made it all the more astounding. Mary couldn't begin to speculate what had changed between the tearful speech Susan had given to celebrate her one-year milestone at CHAOP and the moment she'd decided to shoot BDSM porn. Whatever had occurred, the possibilities were both distressing and intriguing.

"I still can't make sense of it," said a distraught Sister Angela. "I've been praying about it all morning. I've looked at it from every possible angle."

"Not sure some angles should be scrutinized here," Mary said, still fixated on the video.

"Susan made so much progress in this program. All those tearful confessions…all that intensive therapy… Why would she just throw it all away?"

"Are you asking me? You think I know something you don't?"

"I'm hoping for any kind of insight at this point," said Sister Angela. "I knew she had intimacy issues. She even shared those issues with the entire group."

"I don't remember her talking about this kind of intimacy," Mary said.

"Which makes this…this relapse of hers all the more troubling," she said.

The older woman was having a hard time wrapping her head around what had happened. Mary could hardly blame her. Sister Angela had praised Susan's progress time and again, holding her up as an example to others in the program. Now she was more a cautionary tale than a success story.

As the nun continued to pace, Mary finally tore herself away from the video and closed the laptop. She gazed toward the part of the room where the program conducted its meetings, focusing on the exact spot where Susan had stood just a few weeks before. This relapse, as Sister Angela called it, put Mary's ongoing struggles into a whole new context.

The notion that this program was working for everyone else except her had been shattered. The misery and doubt that Mary had been experiencing lately no longer felt odd. How many other recovering sex addicts had these kinds of relapses? How many of them manifested like this in spite of the program? Was it possible that these outbursts of sexual excess manifested *because* of the program? These were important questions to consider, because the answers were sure to affect Mary at some point.

She continued contemplating them as Sister Angela stopped pacing and retrieved the laptop. She then gave Mary one of the skewering glares that only a nun could give.

"That brings me to the second reason I called you — and you alone — to discuss this," she said.

"Oh boy," groaned Mary under her breath.

"There's no need for dread. I'm not going to interrogate you or anything. Tell me that you haven't engaged in any *perverse* activities and I'll believe you."

"I haven't, but that's not the point here, is it?" Mary said.

"No. It isn't."

Sister Angela set the laptop aside and sat down in the chair next to her. That penetrating gaze of hers waned. She once again became the woman who tried to be everybody's friend. It made her difficult to hate. Mary didn't bother trying, letting the nun reach over and grasp her hand, as if to keep her from running away.

"Mary, you've come so far since you joined this program," said Sister Angela, as sincere as anyone could be. "I still remember what led you here. I also remember how angry you were at yourself."

"And I was *this* close to forgetting," Mary said dryly.

"I know it's been hard, sticking to this program and all its tenants. Even with my decadent background, I won't claim I understand what you've been through."

"*That* would be a first."

"But this situation with Susan troubles me because you're coming up on the same milestone. At the end of this week, you'll have been in this program for a full year. I don't think I need to remind you how important that is. In the history of this program, over eighty-five percent of those who make it that far don't relapse."

"Or maybe they're just smart enough *not* to put it on camera," Mary said.

"I'm serious, Mary. I'm worried about you."

"I'm serious, too...at least partially."

The nun squeezed her hand and gave her that penetrating gaze again. This time Mary didn't avoid her scrutiny. Sister Angela was genuinely concerned. She looked at her as though Mary were standing on the edge of a cliff, just waiting for a reason to jump. She might not be entirely wrong, either.

"Mary, a few weeks ago, I saw you sit in this very room and glare at Susan as though she'd run over your dog," Sister Angela continued. "You were tense, uptight, frustrated. You had more reasons to get up and walk away than anyone that night."

"I was having a bad day. Actually, I'd had a streak of bad days going," admitted Mary.

"Which is why I'm so worried about you. At some point, even a strong soul will crack under the strain."

"You think I'm going to relapse, don't you?"

"I think your soul is more vulnerable than most," said Sister Angela.

"So what does that mean for me? Is it only a matter of time before someone sends you a link to some video of me fucking an entire college frat house?"

"I don't believe that. I hope you don't believe that, either. I still have faith in you—in *everyone* to overcome their demons. I just think you're more vulnerable than most because you've struggled more to confront those demons."

Now it felt like Sister Angela was psychoanalyzing her. Nun or not, Mary hated it when anyone did that. That was why she'd chosen this program instead of intense, one-on-one therapy. As much as Mary hated it, though, the older woman still made a valid point.

"When you first joined the program, you had already taken the hardest step," said the older woman. "You'd uprooted your comfortable life of debauchery, moved back to Hartman County and removed yourself from that toxic environment. Many people don't have the strength to do something that drastic."

"Or the incentive," Mary said under her breath.

"Your reasons don't matter. What matters is that you took that step. You put yourself on this path to recovery. It's the next hard step that you've yet to take."

"And which step is that?" Mary asked.

"One I thought Susan had taken but, sadly, I was wrong," replied Sister Angela. "You see, I spoke to her the day before she claimed she had overcome her addiction. Her spirits were high. She was smiling and full of energy. At one point, I asked her how it felt to confront the scars that had driven her addiction. She responded vaguely, but I remembered her spirit *faltering* at that point. I didn't think much of it, but now that I look back, I think it was a sign."

"And are you seeing that same sign in me right now?"

"Honestly, I'm not sure what I see in you, Mary. I suspect you don't know what you see in yourself. Why else would you be so frustrated?"

"You know, one of my old fitness coaches said something similar. I punched him in the gut. I don't like people assuming they know what I think and why I think it."

"I'm not assuming anything, Mary...although I thank you for not punching me," said Sister Angela with a touch of humor.

Mary didn't like this. It would've been the best possible time for someone to pull a fire alarm or something, but she continued to endure. She tried in vain to hide her discomfort while under this woman's gaze. At the same time, she couldn't help but be intrigued by her words.

For most of her life, Mary hadn't scrutinized why she did what she did. All too often, she focused on setting goals, accomplishing those goals and enjoying herself along the way. Realizing that she was a sex addict had forced her to look at herself differently. Getting to that realization had been hard enough. Dealing with it was infinitely harder and

Sister Angela seemed intent on kick-starting that process.

"I don't think Susan fully confronted the scars that drove her addiction. That's why she wasn't able to overcome her deviant impulses. She may have made them *worse* by claiming she'd overcome them," said Sister Angela.

"That or she was just really, *really* horny," Mary said.

"Reckless impulses are very different from basic instincts. That's the first thing we teach in this program. You're strong enough to resist those impulses, Mary. I know that doing so has cost you. I imagine it has made things very difficult for you and your family."

"With all due respect, Sister, I'd rather *not* talk about that," Mary said in a more serious tone.

"I wasn't going to, but what happened with them is a big part of what's happening to you right now. All these things — these issues that make you so uncomfortable — they provided the fuel that drove your addiction. Even if you're not acting on that addiction anymore, it's still driving you. I'm sure it has affected you in ways you don't want to talk about. I've no desire to ask about it, either."

That came as a major relief to Mary. She would rather not tell a nun that she had been masturbating to thoughts of fire and Peter Rogers. Even so, it helped make Sister Angela's point. Her addiction was still present and still very powerful.

"At the end of this week, you might be able to stand up in this room and tell everyone you've been in this program for a year. You might even be able to tell them it's been a year since you last had sex," said Sister Angela.

"I'd rather keep some of those details to myself," Mary said.

"But if you don't confront the source of what drives your addiction, you'll *never* be able to overcome it," said the nun. "The longer you draw it out, the worse it'll get. What you just saw with Susan... It was an extreme example, but it wasn't as extreme as it could've been."

"I don't doubt that. Even my mind isn't *that* dirty."

"And I'd rather not see something like that happen with you. So between now and our next meeting, if you have a chance to deal with something important, I urge you to make the effort. I'll even help you in any way I can."

Sister Angela squeezed her hand a little harder, as if to keep her from joining Susan in her relapsed decadence. She squeezed so hard that it actually hurt, giving Mary even more incentive to take this seriously.

"That's...nice of you, Sister Angela. I'm just...not entirely sure what you're asking me to do here," Mary said.

"I'm not asking you to do anything specifically. I'm just praying you'll find the strength to confront the source of your problems. That's the only way you'll overcome your addiction," said Sister Angela. "I know the temptation you feel is strong. Your ability to resist it must be stronger. Susan overestimated her strength. Don't make the same mistake."

"Believe me, I don't want to. I'd rather not have my sexual proclivities immortalized on the Internet."

"That's just it. I believe you. That's why I challenge you to do something more between now and the end of the week."

"Something *more*? Like what?" Mary asked.

"I wish I could tell you, but you're going to have to figure that out for yourself," said the woman. "Look at the life you've lived. Look at the decisions you've made. Think about it. Pray on it. Dare to probe those wounds that drove you into the arms of addiction. You may not understand it completely. You may not be ready to confront it, but you'll be able to say you made the effort. That's more than Susan can claim."

Mary saw a lot of distress in Sister Angela. Susan relapsing like this had really bothered the woman. She'd thought she had another success story for the Chapman Hill Addiction Outreach Program. Now she wanted Mary to be that story. It put a lot of pressure on her at a time when Mary had a lot to deal with.

Finally, Sister Angela let go of her hand. She clutched the rosary beads she wore on her wrist and prayed, as she often did when she got worked up. While Mary rubbed her sore hand, she thought about this challenge.

Since Peter had come back into her life, she'd given a lot less thought to her upcoming milestone. He had definitely been a helpful distraction in some ways and a not-so-helpful distraction in others. Now, in light of this recent development with Susan, Peter's influence on her gained greater urgency.

These wounds that drive me to addiction... Do I really want to open them again? she asked herself.

It sounded so unappealing and risky, digging into the dark corners of her life that she had been avoiding for nearly a year now. She'd moved back to Hartman County to escape those painful memories. Mary didn't see how any good could possibly come from confronting them. However, Sister Angela had made it sound like the only way for her to get what she wanted out of the program.

Mary didn't see eye-to-eye with Sister Angela on a lot of things about treating addiction, but she saw the merit of some extra introspection. A few weeks ago, she had been in a state where she could've relapsed like Susan, albeit in a far less *kinky* sort of way. Then, Peter had showed up and changed everything. She had been torn between running from her addiction and confronting the emptiness within her. At some point, she had to stop running.

Then, as Sister Angela prayed, a strange thought came to Mary. Sister Angela talked about confronting the driving force behind her addiction, but to some extent, Mary had already made that effort.

By re-connecting with Peter, she'd become more comfortable in her own skin than she had been at any time in her adult life. Perhaps that was a sign. Maybe she had the key to understanding her addiction and didn't even know it. If that were the case, then why not see where it led?

"Sister Angela...I think I'll take you up on that challenge," Mary said with renewed confidence.

"Glad to hear it, Mary. Just know that you have my faith

and support," said Sister Angela.

"You *might* want to give me half for now," Mary said as she got up and walked toward the exit. "What I intend to do involves taking chances that most recovering sex addicts shouldn't take."

"You're being very coy with your tone. Is there something else I should know?"

"I'm sorry, but for the reward to be worth the risk, I need to keep this personal. Don't worry, though. This isn't something the program explicitly forbids."

"I'm still worried," said Sister Angela.

"That makes two of us, but for once…I *actually* have faith that something good might come of it," replied Mary as she took her leave. "If it works, rest assured I'll have plenty to share at our next meeting."

"And if it doesn't?"

Mary stopped at the door and turned back for a brief moment. Sister Angela was still concerned. She couldn't blame her. She had no idea what Mary had been doing with Peter. In order for Mary to do this, she needed to take a chance with him while taking an even *bigger* chance on herself. That meant testing her faith in a way that even a nun couldn't understand.

"Let's just say there are different kinds of relapses," answered Mary, being purposefully vague. "One kind means I'll need to be in this program for *way* more than a year. The other? Well, that depends on what I find when I confront an old part of my life I thought I'd ruined."

Chapter Eleven

Hartman County was no stranger to droughts. Having grown up here, Mary remembered more than a few. The locals had a saying. It went something like, '*The rains only come after the people get used to dry winds.*' In many respects, it was a fitting metaphor for her personal life since leaving Miami.

Before her addiction had ruined her life, Mary had had an abundance of friends, lovers and flings. She'd lived in a city where she could gorge on every kind of social excess. Then she'd left that life and had entered an arid, isolated world where her problems lay completely exposed. By keeping them exposed, Mary reminded herself of the darker parts of that former life. It might have been a fertile valley of self-indulgence, but it had come dangerously close to destroying her.

For a time, her life had seemed destined for two paths. Either she would drown in her addiction or she would wither in her efforts to run from it. Neither path was all that appealing, but until recently, she hadn't seen any alternatives.

Now, she was convinced that there had to be a third path. Finding it meant more than just taking a chance. Mary also had to get someone else to take a chance with her, because this was one of those challenges that nobody could confront on their own.

"Well, *this* get-together is a wash, so to speak," Peter said restlessly.

"In the middle of a record drought, that's in terrible taste, Peter," Mary said.

"It sounded good on paper. Hang out near the waterpark during Summer Family Fun Day. All the little kids and beleaguered parents running around... It's the exact *opposite* of South Beach."

"You might have been right. I guess we'll never know. Somehow the county ordered every public pool to shut down to conserve water and you—a guy who *works* for the county, no less—didn't know about it."

"In my defense, I don't keep up with city politics," Peter said.

"Too late. I hold *you* personally responsible for this," Mary said.

Peter rolled his eyes and laughed. He seemed relieved but concerned. This setting undermined the rules they'd laid out when they'd started doing this. They were supposed to only meet in open, public areas where they wouldn't be tempted to get too intimate. Sitting at a picnic table just outside a waterpark during a family event definitely fit that criteria, but circumstances beyond their control had gotten in the way.

With the waterpark closed due to the drought, Mary and Peter sat alone at a picnic table with nothing but the late afternoon sun watching over them. They saw a couple of workers inside the closed park, but nothing that could effectively kill the mood if things got heated. It made Peter uncomfortable, but Mary saw it as a blessing in disguise. For what she had in mind, being alone with him might work better.

"If you want, we can try going somewhere else. I'm guessing the mall is packed on a day like this," Peter said.

"That's okay. I'm fairly comfortable here," Mary said.

"Here in the blazing summer heat with a guy who happens to be a recovering sex addict...alone?" he asked. "Are you really *that* confident in our ability to keep our clothes on?"

"As confident as I can be...and some of those circumstances are less tempting than you think."

"What do you mean?"

Mary shifted uncomfortably, having dreaded this moment. She really didn't care about where she and Peter had agreed to meet this time. They could've met in an alley behind a fast food restaurant for all she cared. She just needed him in a place where he could listen.

"Peter, we've been doing this for a couple of weeks now. And make no mistake, it has made a *huge* difference," Mary said. "I haven't felt this comfortable in my own skin since I left Miami. Just re-connecting with someone — being close to them in a way I haven't allowed myself to be... It means a *lot* to me. And, let's face it, there's only so much connection you can have with co-workers, customers and family members who think sex addiction is a joke."

"I appreciate the sentiment, but I'm expecting some fine print," Peter said.

"Don't make this into a hostage negotiation. I'm saying this because it needs to be said. What we've been doing *isn't* innocuous. It may seem that way — hanging out at public places and talking about work, politics or the weather — but it's not. It *means* something and I don't think we should shrug it off."

Mary put more emotion into those words than she'd intended. She'd promised herself she would keep her feelings in check. She'd expected to break that promise to some degree, but not this early. It sent a clear message to Peter, who quickly took notice.

"I don't disagree with anything you just said, but you're giving me the impression there's something wrong with that picture," Peter said.

"There *is* in the sense that what we have is...incomplete," Mary said. "That day at the softball game when this all began, you opened some old wounds that you didn't want to expose. But you did and, unless you're keeping secrets from me, it really helped."

"It did," Peter said. "As for me keeping secrets? Well, you remember how much I sucked at keeping secrets as a kid. Don't expect me to be any better as an adult."

"It also forced you to be brutally honest. I can see now why women loved you."

"Mary, I thought you were being serious."

"I *am*, Peter. This is probably the most serious I've been in the past year," Mary said. "You made yourself vulnerable to me, just like you did with so many women in the past. And, well...I haven't returned the favor. I haven't opened *my* wounds for you and that's just not fair — to either of us."

She let Peter make the connections from there. It didn't take long and, just as Mary expected, he got very uncomfortable for a new set of reasons.

Peter had told her about the fateful moment where his addiction became too much, but Mary hadn't shared her pivotal moment. He hadn't asked either, nor did she expect him to. Peter had confronted one too many painful emotions by telling her his story. He probably didn't have the stomach for more, but she needed him to work up the appetite.

As her intentions became clear, Peter rubbed his neck awkwardly and looked out toward the closed waterpark. Unlike before, they had no distractions to help them. That magnified the risks but created new opportunities, and he didn't seem eager to embrace those.

"I thought we agreed we weren't ready for this," Peter said.

"We never agreed on anything. We never even discussed it," Mary pointed out.

"It was sort of implied...avoiding unpleasant topics," he said, "primarily the thing that turned you from a free-spirit to a full-blown sex addict."

"Others just called me a slut, but thanks for tweaking your words."

"Does it matter what I call it? I've never pressured you to tell me what happened. I gather that it was bad — so bad, in fact, that you abandoned a promising modeling career in Miami and moved back to Hartman County."

"Trust me, it's worse than bad," Mary said. "I've only

dropped passing hints. You might not have picked up on a few."

"I assume there's a good reason for that and I don't want you to share those reasons just because I spilled my guts. That wouldn't be fair," Peter said.

"You tell me your secrets, but I don't tell you mine? How is that fair?"

"You know what I mean, Mary. You know why we've been so careful. Can you honestly look me in the eye and tell me you're ready for something like this?"

If he had asked her that question a day ago, she would've said no without an ounce of hesitation. After her conversation with Sister Angela, however, Mary had given it more thought. The situation had changed and so had her answer.

With far less hesitation than Peter probably expected, Mary grasped his chin and turned his head so that she could look him in the eye, just as he'd asked her to do.

"Yes, I'm ready," Mary said definitively. "Are you?"

"Of...of course I am," replied Peter anxiously. "You know I'm here for you, Mary, but—"

She silenced him by raising her hand, avoiding any chance for him to talk her out of this.

"It's a touchy subject, I know," she said. "It's going to open old wounds, stir up old feelings and make things *very* awkward. I understand all of that. But I've been thinking lately and I really, really want to share this with you. In fact, I *need* to share it with you."

Mary made sure she emphasized that need, still caressing his face so Peter could see the certainty in her eyes. He got the message loud and clear.

"Okay, then. If you want to tell me this, I'll listen. I can't guarantee I'm going to say all the right things...or that it won't get awkward," Peter said.

"I'll endure. I don't need you to understand. I just want you to listen and trust me," Mary said.

"You know, you're not the first beautiful woman to ask

me that. And I should warn you there are times when I've been burned by those exact words."

"Then I'll have to make this the exception. I'll have to because there's something else I want to tell you afterward — something that might complicate things even more."

"So why don't we stick to one complication at a time, then? Let's not make it any harder than it has to be," Peter said, already sounding overwhelmed.

Despite her intent, Mary nodded and released her grip on him. She also gave him some extra space to mitigate any awkwardness she had already caused.

They still had an unspoken rule that they wouldn't get too touchy with one another, out of concern that it might rile up their hormones in all the wrong ways. They had already broken a few of those rules. They couldn't break too many of them too quickly. That would just make things harder. But if breaking that many rules was necessary, then Mary expected to bear most of that burden.

Bracing herself for that, she settled in for a very personal, very painful story. That gave Peter a chance to get comfortable as well. Now giving her his full attention, he had no idea that he already understood her story better than most.

"I'll start with the easy parts," began Mary. "You left for Los Angeles while my life continued here in Hartman County. I doubt you'll be surprised by how that life unfolded. A potent combination of exercise, youthful energy and puberty gave me a growth spurt in all the right places. By the time I was fifteen, I filled out bras better than most of the girls in my class. By sixteen, I was filling out thongs as well."

"You're right. I'm not surprised," Peter said. "You were never shy about your looks."

"I was even less shy about taking advantage of them. As soon as hormonal boys started noticing me, I noticed them back. I didn't take it slowly, either. I gave my first blow job when I was fifteen. I had full-on, all nude, virginity-killing sex when I was sixteen — the day after my birthday, no less. I got my first taste of anal a year later."

"Giving or receiving?" Peter said, half-jokingly.

"Both," Mary said flatly.

That effectively killed Peter's efforts to keep this conversation from getting too serious, but it helped make Mary's point. Peter, having shared his own sexual history with her, offered no harsh judgment. He just kept listening.

"I won't deny it. I was a slut, plain and simple," Mary said flatly. "I wasn't ashamed of it, though. I'm *still* not ashamed. I love sex. Being the classic high school hottie, I had plenty of opportunities to enjoy it. In a town like this — which might as well be the antithesis of LA — I didn't have a lot of competition. I essentially had *all* the leverage. I could have any guy I wanted and do with him whatever the hell I wanted."

"Did it ever get serious?" Peter asked.

"In terms of relationships? No, I never let it. I guess this is where you and I were on the same wavelength. You didn't want to be tied down. I made it clear to every guy before my panties came off that I wasn't looking for a boyfriend. I just wanted a good fuck."

"Can't imagine they complained," Peter said. "I can't imagine they were completely okay with it, either. Did it ever get dangerous?"

"Nope. I didn't let that happen," Mary said. "I guess I forged my own path there. I didn't want to be one of those traditional sluts who just used her ass to make life more comfortable. I still wanted to work for something. I still wanted a future that I could say I earned."

"You're right. That's hardly traditional for an admitted slut. I bet your family was so proud."

"Funny you should mention that, because this is where they played a major role...for better *and* for worse."

She still hadn't told Peter anything she hadn't already told Sister Angela. Mary didn't sugarcoat this part of her past. In fact, it in her life was the most innocent, so to speak. That concept clashed with her admission to being an unapologetic slut, but sex itself didn't make her an addict. There were other factors involved in that exceedingly painful process.

"Don't get the wrong idea. I didn't become a slut because of daddy issues or any of that shit you hear on daytime talk shows," Mary said.

"I knew your dad, Mary. You don't need to convince me of that," Peter said.

"That alone sets you apart, because a lot of people *love* to make that assumption. The truth is rarely that predictable, but it probably wouldn't shock anyone, either," she continued. "If anyone influenced my love of dick, it was my brothers...and not in the way you think."

"I wasn't thinking it. I promise," Peter said, putting his hands up in defense.

"Thanks, because a lot of people assume the worst. The reality is that having two older brothers who happened to be big, strong, womanizing brutes put me in a testosterone-heavy environment from birth. Before I started filling out bras, I saw them hooking up with pretty girls and discussing female anatomy in ways that would make my old health teacher blush. My dad — having fooled around plenty in his youth — didn't hide it from me. So as soon as I was curious enough to ask about it, he told me what sex was, how to do it and how to do it right."

"I want to say that's weird, but I know your dad was never all that uptight," Peter said.

"He wasn't, and for anything he glossed over, my brothers helped fill in any gaps. So, when the time came for to put myself out there, I was way more equipped than most," Mary said. "I knew how to use condoms and birth control. I knew how to tell if a guy was lying. So, while other girls were getting knocked up or getting their hearts broken, I was enjoying every kind of safe, healthy, carefree sex."

It was strange, but not as much as it should've been. Mary remembered those times fondly. Sex had been so much easier back then. She had just attracted the guys she wanted, made her intentions clear and let raging hormones do the rest. Like so many other parts of her youth, though, it hadn't stayed simple. In addition, there had been warning signs that she had put herself on a dangerous path.

"For a while, it was like an arms race," she continued. "While my brothers fooled around with all these women, I tried to match their foolishness with men."

"You always were pretty competitive," Peter said.

"That's a good trait to have for someone with a career in athletics. For sibling rivalries...not so much. My brothers didn't encourage it, but they didn't exactly discourage it, either. They didn't see me as their sister, the slut. They saw me as their sister, the tough young woman who could hold her own against any man."

"Including sex?"

"*Especially* sex," Mary said. "Being tough didn't just mean being an athlete. It meant never losing control of a situation. I guess after my mom died that we all needed to be a little tougher. I just had to go the extra mile. I think that might have been the first sign."

"Yeah, but everybody overlooks that first one," Peter said.

He made a valid point. Mary didn't beat herself up too much for not seeing it then, but that didn't make her choices back then any less egregious.

"You might be right, but I *really* pushed it," Mary said with a sigh. "After high school, my brothers and I drifted apart. They went to college on athletic scholarships. I went to community college because I had different plans. They had to get their act together to pursue their goals, but I didn't. I kept hooking up with random guys just as I always had—like I had something to prove."

"I think you more than made your point," commented Peter.

"Funny, my brothers told me the same thing. I must have shrugged it off because I didn't stop. Then, my father died and things started to escalate."

Her tone shifted and she tensed. It was the part of her story that Mary hadn't shared with Sister Angela. If Peter hadn't known her, she probably could've skipped this part and gotten away with it. However, he already knew parts of her story and it wouldn't have conveyed the full impact if she skipped it.

It was another one of those ominous signs she'd overlooked, but this one was more egregious. She could blame her behavior on being a hormonal teenager only to a point. Being a competent adult meant Mary had fewer excuses.

"Was this the turning point for you?" Peter asked, before the silence got too awkward.

"No. Not entirely," answered Mary. "It was devastating. Don't get me wrong. Liver disease is *not* the way my dad wanted to go. I imagine he wanted to die driving a hot rod off the Grand Canyon while a bunch of cheerleaders in bikinis cheered him on. However, it happened, and it caught me and my brothers totally off-guard."

"Yeah, death is pretty good at that."

"And I didn't respond as well as I could've. Mourning him was hard enough. The logistical issues though… Those tore my family apart."

"And now I'm sorry I wasn't there for you," Peter said. "I remember finding out your dad had died. If I'd have known how bad it was, I would've flown in and helped."

"That's sweet of you, Peter, but believe me, there's *nothing* you could've done," Mary said solemnly. "Even before the funeral, we argued over his inheritance. You see, the auto body shop that my dad spent his whole life building had been in trouble. I don't know the specifics, but my dad had apparently hired some inept employees—and not just the kind who left a few bolts loose."

"How inept did things get?"

"That, I don't know. I just know that after he died, some chain store wanted to buy it. At the time, I thought 'why not'? The money they offered was pretty good. I certainly needed it. The only problem was my brothers wanted to maintain the business. They thought selling it while our father's body was still warm was just plain wrong. I thought keeping a failing business alive was worse."

"I can see both sides. I can also see you being *very* stubborn about your position."

"Then I don't have to convince you that I drove a wedge between me and my brothers," Mary said. "Hell, I'm pretty sure I burned every bridge I could possibly burn with them. I ended up negotiating behind their backs, striking a deal that was more on *my* terms and not theirs."

"You've always been a good negotiator, Mary. Those terms must have been pretty good."

"It didn't matter how good they were. It didn't matter that I got them more money than the initial offer. My brothers *still* got pissed, but they had no choice to sign off on it. We all walked away with a hefty lump sum. We were bitter, but richer. Then, the shop went out of business a few years later. So, in the end, I was vindicated."

"I doubt that mattered to them," Peter said.

"It didn't," affirmed Mary. "It just gave me a damn good excuse to get away from my family and out of Hartman County. I dropped out of community college, took my money and started a new life in Miami. I had no family support. I also had a lot of bitterness and angst to work through. And keep in mind, I was still a beautiful young woman with a great rack and a nice ass. I had a lot of *opportunities* for seeking comfort."

She let Peter use his imagination to fill in the sordid details, to let more connections fall into place, the path that had led her back to Hartman County as a jaded sex addict to become a bit clearer. However, even his perverse imagination couldn't comprehend just how bad it had gotten.

In recalling those turbulent times in her life, some old emotions welled up inside her. A hard lump formed in her throat, adding more strain to the painful recollection.

Knowing it would get a lot worse before it got better, she kept going, hoping her emotions couldn't keep up.

"Stop me if this sounds too familiar," continued Mary. "I was a young, beautiful, horny woman in a town full of nightclubs, rich tourists and topless beaches. I was also emotionally wounded and looking to treat those wounds with every kind of indulgence. Then, I encountered plenty of equally beautiful, equally horny men willing to oblige me — not forgetting, mind you, that I was still in the mindset that I had to be tough in all things, including sex."

"It's familiar, but not *too* familiar," Peter said.

"On top of that, I started a career that put me into contact with more beautiful people. I took that tainted inheritance money and build a gym right on South Beach. I built it up into one of the most successful gyms in the city, getting attention from a modeling agency in the process. That put me into contact with even more beautiful people, men and women alike."

"Men *and* women?"

"Don't pretend to be shocked. When you've got so many options, you tend to take a dip in the other side of the pool," Mary said, rolling her eyes.

"Did I say I disapproved?" retorted Peter.

"Just don't imagine anything too pornographic. It wasn't like that...for the most part."

"Then just how bad did it get? With all those opportunities, there had to be a point where you noticed."

His insight was uncanny. Nobody who hadn't gone through a similar experience would make that assumption. They were usually too busy imagining her various acts of sexual excess, which often derailed any attempts at having this sort of conversation with someone else. Mary didn't doubt that some unpleasant images had crossed Peter's mind, but he continued to listen. That made staying ahead of her emotions even more difficult.

"I want to say you're pushing it, but when you're right, damn it if you aren't right," Mary said.

"You can give me the PG-13 version if you want," assured Peter.

"That still wouldn't do it justice. You didn't gloss over the details when you told me about your promiscuity, so why should I? I basically ran around Miami, screwing anything that looked like it could screw back. I'd fuck guys at my gym, I'd fuck them at clubs and I'd fuck them in restaurant bathrooms. I wasn't passive about it, either. If I'd see someone I wanted to screw, I'd pursue them, tell them what I wanted and how I wanted to do it. Most of the time, they agreed. If they didn't, I'd tempt them. I used every bit of leverage I had to make sure I got something out of it."

"Sounds like you were...aggressive," commented Peter.

"I was. Again, I didn't think about it at the time. It was just how I did things. Even after the pain of my father's death had passed, I kept doing it. That means I didn't let myself fall in love. I didn't let myself get too emotionally attached. I just stayed focused, riding the success of my gym and my modeling career and anyone I wanted to fuck along the way."

"In other words, you tried to do what I did. It was just easier for you."

"With boobs like mine? Yeah, it probably was," admitted Mary. "There was nothing that could stop me—nothing that could convince me I had a problem. I didn't think I was hurting myself or anyone else. I never even contemplated that it could. That all changed when..."

She had to stop. Her emotions had finally caught up with her. Despite her best efforts, Mary couldn't escape them. The growing lump in her throat became a stabbing pain. All the burdens she'd carried suddenly felt much heavier. She tried to steady her breathing to stop herself from crying, but it was no use.

Peter reached over to comfort her, but Mary didn't accept it. She just stared down at the ground, her lips quivering and her eyes welling up with tears. She wiped them away, smearing her makeup and undermining the beauty that had once enticed so many. It was somewhat fitting, her emotions making her feel ugly. Fate, it seemed, wouldn't let her forget the pain she'd caused herself and others.

"It's okay, Mary. We can stop for a while if you want," assured Peter.

"No. I *need* to tell you this. I need to tell you for the same reason you told me," Mary said, still fighting her tears.

"You don't have to if you're not ready. If you don't think I'll understand—"

"That's just it, Peter," she said, stopping him in mid-sentence. "You probably understand better than anyone on this planet right now. I've never been able to talk to anyone about this. Not my friends, not my brothers, not Sister Angela—*anybody*!"

"Why? What is it?" he asked intently.

She still struggled to get it out. For a brief moment, Mary contemplated getting up and walking away. This was *much* harder than she'd thought. However, she didn't dare back down. She was tougher than this. Sexual addiction hadn't changed that. Besides, Peter deserved to know the truth. He deserved to know what had led her to this moment.

"Because I did the same thing you did," she answered. "I killed somebody."

Chapter Twelve

Mary prepared herself for any number of reactions. After what she'd just told Peter, there weren't many that would surprise her. He might be shocked. He might be horrified. He might even burst out laughing over the irony after having told her the *exact* same thing a few weeks ago. Anything would've been appropriate at this point. However, nothing could've prepared her for the cold silence that followed.

After saying those fateful words, every bit of ambient noise around seemed muted. Mary could no longer hear the wind blowing through the trees, the birds chirping or the people working in the closed waterpark across the street. It was as if the entire world had become frozen, leaving only her and Peter to confront this moment.

Agonizing over every second of silence, Mary felt ready to burst. She began to question whether she had the strength to get through it all.

Finally, Peter said something. "Damn," was all that came out.

It wasn't much, but it kept Mary from going over the edge. Still staring at the ground, she scoffed at him.

"Really? That's all you have to say?" Mary said, bemused by his response. "Then again, maybe that's the best I can hope for."

"No, it's not. I'm sorry if that sounded…off," stammered Peter.

"Don't be. It's not like there's a right way to react. Hell, I proved that when you told me the same thing."

"Yeah, I don't disagree. I'm just…trying to wrap my head around this so I can respond in a way that won't piss you off."

"Believe me, I'd rather be pissed right now," Mary said.

"And since I can't lie worth a damn, I guess we're past that point. To be honest, I'm really curious now. This puts your reaction to my confession in a whole new context, but I don't want to assume too much. I'll just expect there were...circumstances."

She still tried to get mad at him, but his sincere, wanting gaze of his was on her. She hadn't been able to resist it when they had been kids. She had no hope of avoiding it now.

Frustration helped temper her emotions. Mary adjusted herself, attempting to salvage what remained of her strength. She turned back to face Peter, still clearly surprised by her admission. That might change once she told him the painful details.

"You know, sometimes I hate how understanding you are, Peter," Mary said.

"You're not the first beautiful woman to tell me that," he said with a half-grin.

"I'm sure that got you laid almost as much as your washboard abs and toned biceps. But as much as I hate it at times, I need that understanding right now."

"Does that mean the circumstances were similar or just the results?" Peter asked.

"I'm not sure. To be honest, I've tried very hard not to think about those *circumstances* for the past year. Needless to say, I failed miserably. You might pick up on some similarities, but keep in mind that my approach to sex was different from yours. You didn't just rely on your looks. You used charm, understanding and dedication to get women out of their panties and into your bed. Aside from looks, I took a more direct approach. I saw a guy I wanted to fuck, I seduced him and I made sure I enjoyed the hell out of it."

"Not sure that approach would've worked for me. Hell, it probably would've gotten me arrested."

"I guess we can chalk that up to fucked-up double standards." Mary shrugged. "A girl who's aggressive at getting guys into bed is just a slut. A guy who's just as aggressive is a restraining order waiting to happen. For a beautiful woman who also happened to be an aspiring fitness model? Well, let's just say I had a *lot* more leeway."

"I'm sure you did, but how does that lead you to killing someone?" Peter asked.

"It's actually not that hard when you're in the process of becoming a full-blown sex addict. In my case, I accelerated that process. I wasn't just fooling around and enjoying my youth. I was feeding an actual need. I didn't just restrict it to clubs or gym rats, either. In the same way I push myself when I work out, I pushed myself in the variety of men I seduced."

"I'm not entirely sure what that entails, but I can make a few educated guesses."

"And they'd only be half-right, at best," Mary said.

It might have been a good idea to skip those details. They'd come from the most reckless, depraved part of her life. She wasn't proud of those times. It still pained her to dwell on them. However, Peter had been honest and *specific* in admitting the extent of his depravity. At the very least, she had to return the favor.

"As my needs became a full-blown addiction, things escalated pretty quickly," Mary said. "To exercise my growing libido, I made it more challenging on myself. I fucked police officers, aspiring politicians, pastors and even a gym teacher who worked at a local elementary school."

"That doesn't sound too bad," commented Peter.

"Oh, yeah? I once blew the pizza guy in exchange for extra toppings," added Mary.

"Okay, I take it back. It does sound bad."

"And, of course, I didn't see it as a problem. I was way past giving a damn. I didn't care who these men were — or women, in some cases. I didn't care if they were married, in love or had kids. I didn't care if they had any genuine feelings for me, either. I just went after them and got what I wanted. For a while, I was able to handle it. But eventually—as you found out, as well—it *does* catch up to you. Sometimes, it just has to happen in the worst possible way."

"You're right. Sometimes that's what it takes," Peter said. "So, what was his name?"

There was that understanding again. He surmised that this moment involved a name that had been permanently etched in her mind, just as Gabriel Anderson had been etched in his. He wasn't entirely wrong, so she didn't bother getting upset. In fact, he'd made it easier.

There were still many painful emotions burning inside her, but some of those emotions faded under Peter's gaze. He gave no harsh judgments or criticisms. He remained serious and concerned as a friend, not just as someone taking in the depravity of a self-professed sex addict. For Mary, who hadn't shared the full story with anybody before now, he couldn't have carried himself any better. Now, she had to do the same.

"The man's full name was Mark Steven Howard," Mary said. "He'd moved to South Florida as a teenager. He had good parents, went to a top school and made a decent living as an up-and-coming lawyer. He also married his high school sweetheart, was active in his church and had a couple of adorable kids. Their names are David and Gwen."

"Sounds like you've done your research on this guy. I'm not sure that's healthy," Peter said.

"It isn't. Believe me, I know it isn't. But before I knew anything about this man's life, he was just another man I'd slept with," Mary said. "I didn't really see it as that big a challenge. I had a few parking tickets on my record. Someone at the gym gave me his card, saying he could get them wiped clean. I met with him, talked to him and decided I wanted to have sex with him."

"There *had* to be signs, though. You wouldn't remember it this clearly if there weren't."

"You'd be right, and I still want to punch myself for not seeing them. Mark wasn't as...eager to cheat on his wife as most men. He made it clear that he really loved her. I made it clear that I didn't want to change that. I just wanted sex. I didn't stop and think that maybe seducing a happily married man was a bad idea. I just remembered leaning over his desk, showing a little extra cleavage and making it clear to him what I wanted."

"And that was enough?"

"We were in motel room in less than twenty minutes," replied Mary. "He was...passive. I could tell that on some level he felt guilty. I didn't care. That had never stopped me before. That just meant I had to be more assertive. I stripped him where he stood. Then, I gave him a little lap dance to ease his guilt, so to speak. He didn't say much after that. He just laid back on the bed, I got on top of him and we did what we did."

"And that's all there was to it?" Peter said.

"It was enough. I still got what I wanted," Mary said. "I even told him it could be our little secret. Nobody ever had to know. I just assumed he agreed because I got out of bed, got dressed and left — not expecting to ever see him again."

"How long did *that* last?"

She sensed that Peter had probably pieced together more of the fateful moment already. Like him, she'd brushed aside any signs or reservations after she'd had her way with the man. It reminded her of the attitude he'd described when he told her how he chose to be with that woman instead of respond to a fire alarm. The similarities actually ran much deeper than that.

"It lasted less than twelve hours, if you can believe that," she admitted.

"I believe it. I really wish I didn't, but I do," Peter said.

"After I left that motel, I went home and had my last peaceful night's sleep. The next day, I went to the gym to open up, like I always did. But when I got there, the whole front entrance had been cordoned off by police. There were even a few local reporters gathering outside. Something was going on and — not knowing any better — I went in for a closer look. That's when I saw it."

Sorrow turned to horror as the memory of that fateful moment flashed before her eyes. Mary could still remember the sights, sounds and scents of that instant. Even after all this time, it still felt so intense, as though it had just happened yesterday. It had plagued her ever since and would probably do so until her dying day.

She swallowed a few times in an effort to gather her strength. More tears welled up in her eyes as she fought the need to break down. Peter attempted to comfort her, just as she had done when he'd told her his story. She didn't reject it, but she didn't acknowledge it, either. This was *her* burden. She deserved the torment it brought her.

"That was a Thursday. I always came in a half-hour late on Thursday because I picked up supplies on my way," Mary said through her sobs. "My staff knew this, so Sarah Michael Peterson—this beautiful young woman who taught yoga part-time—worked the front desk. Had I been there on time, I..."

She had to stop for a moment. Her emotions wouldn't let her continue. Tears streamed down her face. Peter tried to wipe them away, but she wouldn't let him.

I deserve this pain. I deserve this sorrow.

Just saying the young girl's name out loud made the image of her appear before Mary's eyes. Then a much more gruesome image flashed before her and her stomach churned almost as much as it had on that fateful day.

"She was *dead*. Shot in the head...murdered...executed," she finally said out loud. "I saw her body lying on the floor, surrounded by a pool of blood. She had been shot...a lot. She had like...nine bullets in her chest. There was so much blood and so much...other stuff."

"I'm a firefighter. I've seen some pretty gruesome shit, Mary. I know how disturbing death can be," Peter said in an effort to show empathy.

"Not like this," Mary said, her lips quivering at the memory. "I'll...I'll never forget that sight—her face frozen with her eyes still open. Then there was that smell — that godawful smell!"

"It's okay. You don't need to be so vivid."

He lightly grasped her arm to dissuade her. This time, Mary didn't shrug him off. She needed someone to pull her back. If she continued, she would've deepened the scars. She couldn't do that to herself. She couldn't do that to Peter, either, making him share the sorrow that was hers to bear.

With Peter's comforting grip on her, Mary managed to regain some strength. She wiped the tears from her eyes and took several deep breaths. The intense imagery of that moment still lingered, but she refused to turn away. She was determined to continue.

"It was Mark's wife. She was the one who pulled the trigger," Mary said, her voice still strained. "Sarah wasn't the target, though. *I* was."

"So...I guess it didn't stay your little secret," Peter said.

"No. It didn't," Mary said, shaking her head solemnly. "According to the cops, he'd gone home that afternoon and sobbingly confessed that he'd slept with another woman. There was a fight — a *big* fight with lots of yelling and crying. At one point, Mark's wife threatened to leave him and take the kids. It pushed him over the edge. That's when Mark went up into his attic, found a Glock nine-millimeter pistol and — "

Mary let Peter fill in the rest. She didn't have the stomach to finish this part of the story. Even Peter, despite his experience as a firefighter, wouldn't be eager to know the details. He just gave her arm a light squeeze and let her continue.

"When she found him lying dead in their bedroom, I guess she just...*snapped*," Mary said, her words doing little justice to the horror. "Can't say I blame her, either. It's not every day the love of your life cheats on you then blows his brains out. She went from a woman who'd never committed a crime in her life to one with murder on her mind."

"So, she blamed you for everything," Peter said.

"And she should've," Mary said. "*I* seduced her husband. *I* destroyed a loving couple and their entire family just because I was horny. It's every bit as crass as it sounds, but she didn't know that. For all she knew, I was trying to run away with the guy. She wasn't going to let me get away with what I'd done, even if he was dead. So, she found where I worked, stood in the parking lot for two hours and waited for someone to open. She didn't have a picture of me. She just knew I was some pretty girl. Sarah fit that description. So, in the end, two more innocent people died because of me."

"Two more?"

"Yeah, did I forget that part? After Mark's wife killed Sarah, she turned the gun on herself," Mary clarified, her voice now full of self-loathing.

"Damn...and here I was thinking it couldn't get much worse," Peter said.

"Funny, I thought the same thing at the time. I guess karma is a fan of overkill," Mary said. "Mark's wife didn't even know that she'd killed the wrong person. She probably died thinking she got her revenge. Instead, there I was, standing outside my gym, watching this terrifying scene that *I* created. You want to talk about a moment of clarity? Well, that is the kind of clarity that makes you want to violently throw up."

"It's also the kind of clarity that reveals the truth in its coldest, hardest form." His tone had shifted. Then Peter let go of her arm and faced her with that penetrating stare of his. It was a gaze she never got from Sister Angela or anyone else from the Chapman Hill Addiction Outreach Program. It was the look from a man who'd experienced that same painful clarity — of someone who'd felt firsthand the weight of the trauma such clarity had wrought.

Mary tried to turn away first, but there was no escaping it. When she finally turned back toward him with tears still streaming down her face, she saw more than just empathy. There was a strange intrigue in his eyes, as though she held the key to something that he had been searching for. Mary wasn't sure what to make of it, but she felt it, too. "You say that like it's a good thing," Mary said.

"It isn't," Peter said.

"So why are you looking at me as if I just said something profound?"

"Because it is," he replied. "I'd even go so far as to say it's more profound than you realize, but I'll wait until you finish. I'm guessing there's more."

"Guessing or assuming?" Mary asked.

"Does it matter?"

There was a distinct certainty in his tone, almost to the point of being smug. Mary chose not to contest it. She would've only proven Peter right. Now curious herself, she gathered what remained of her strength and continued.

Her emotions settled and her tears finally dried up. There was no use crying over it anymore. Mary knew what she had done. She knew what she had become. She'd stopped running from it after that fateful day. Even so, that cold, hard truth had never stopped tormenting her.

"What happened after I saw that body... I want to say it was all a blur, but I wasn't that lucky," Mary said. "The first thing I did was throw up right there on the sidewalk. I think I threw up every meal I'd had for the past three days. One of the police officers actually tried to call an ambulance. I talked him out of it."

"I doubt that wouldn't have done much good," Peter said. "Even morphine only goes so far."

"You're probably right. They didn't even make me give a statement. I just ran home as quickly as I could, drank everything in my kitchen that had alcohol in it and passed out on my living room floor. Keep in mind that this was still early in the morning. I was still bawling my eyes out, but I wasn't crying. I was just so...so horrified that I couldn't process it."

"So you tried to numb it," he surmised.

"And I failed," Mary said. "I woke up seven hours later

with no fewer than twenty missed calls and the worst hangover I've ever had. I stumbled over to my bathroom, took off all my clothes and looked at myself in the mirror. *That's* the moment when it finally sank in."

Mary dropped her head low in sorrow. This time, she didn't cry or sob. She just let the anguish consume her. She felt Peter's penetrating gaze on her, but she didn't try to avoid it. He was still looking for something in her. However, that didn't concern her at the moment. Right now, she needed to complete her confession.

"I was... I *am* responsible for those deaths," continued Mary.

"You didn't pull the trigger. You didn't buy the gun," Peter said.

"You're not the first person to tell me that. You're not even the tenth. As far as the police were concerned, I'd committed no crime. I'd slept with a married man. That'll get you on a few dirty glares and a spot on daytime TV, but it won't get you thrown in jail."

"But that didn't make it any easier, did it?" he said.

"I'm sure people told you the same thing about Gabriel Anderson and his family. That didn't stop you from blaming yourself," Mary said.

"I never said it should."

"Then I don't need to tell you how much it tormented me. I finally had to take a long, hard look at myself. I was a selfish, unapologetic slut who exploited her looks to get what she wanted. I may have come off as an open, outgoing ball of sexy feminine energy, but at my core I was just... cold. It didn't matter who I slept with. It didn't matter how many people I connected with. I just..." Mary's ability to make sense of the situation failed her. She started feeling overwhelmed again. Then, Peter placed his hands on her shoulders and turned her gaze toward his once more.

"You couldn't be intimate with them," he told her. "You could be passionate with them. You could be close with them. You just couldn't be *intimate*."

"Yes, that's...actually pretty accurate," Mary said.

"You finally saw how selfish that was—how *empty* that made you. That emptiness became a scar, the first of many."

"Your accuracy is getting a little scary here, Peter...but not in a bad way."

"I'm sorry if I'm putting words in your mouth," Peter said.

"It's okay. You're saying it way better than I could have. Besides, there isn't much else to add from there. Once I confronted that emptiness, I realized I had a problem. Shortly after that, I also realized I wasn't in a very good environment to solve that problem. I still had all these hot guys around me, ready to give me all the pity sex I wanted."

"You were tempted to accept it, but you held back, didn't you?"

"I want to say you're still scaring me, but I can't say I mind," Mary said. "It's true. I was tempted. Hell, I wanted to just drown my sorrows in all the dicks in Miami, but I knew it would just make me feel worse. I tried reaching out to my brothers, but...let's just say that wasn't an easy conversation. That led me to sell my gym, give up modeling and move back to Hartman County."

"But you didn't come back with a plan," Peter said, making even more connections. "You didn't know how you were going to heal. You didn't know how you were going to deal with the void. You just needed to get away because you didn't trust yourself anymore."

"Okay, now you're scaring me again," Mary said.

"Then look me in the eye and tell me I'm wrong." He said that with complete confidence.

Mary still made the effort, looking at him like he'd asked and trying to get the words out. Again, she failed. However, she didn't mind this time. Instead, her intrigue only grew.

The sentiment must have drawn Peter closer to her. In a bold gesture, he snaked his arms around her and pulled her into a light embrace. It should have triggered the kind of feelings in Mary that had made her leave Miami, but there was something different about this.

Under his penetrating gaze, she felt genuinely vulnerable. However, that wasn't necessarily a bad thing. Peter might be onto something and Mary needed to see where it led.

"You didn't think you could do the right thing for the right reasons. Hell, you didn't even know what the right thing or the right reasons were anymore," Peter said, continuing his thought. "You did what you thought made sense at the time. You *ran*. You ran from the world you'd once embraced. You told yourself it was just to avoid the temptation. Except—"

"That wasn't the only reason. It wasn't even the most *important* reason," Mary said, now making some of those connections as well.

Peter smiled. Her line of thinking was catching up to his. Now, Mary could follow it with him. She still had no idea where it would lead, but she needed to find out.

"So, you've been running now for how long?" Peter asked.

"Almost a year," answered Mary.

"You've tried to rebuild your life while treating this addiction that left you so scarred. Near as I can tell, you've learned to cope. I don't get the impression you've slipped up and dry humped a bartender."

"I haven't...although, believe me, there are times I've wanted to," Mary said.

"If it makes you feel better, I've wanted to bang every pretty waitress I've seen since I moved back to Hartman County."

"It doesn't, but I'm guessing there's something else you're getting at."

"I'm trying. I'm not sure I'm succeeding, but damn it, I'm trying," Peter said, embracing her a little tighter. "In hearing your story and thinking about mine, I see something that I didn't see before—something I think we've both overlooked."

"Well, what is it?" Mary asked intently, clutching him as

though Peter were her last hope.

"I'm still trying to figure it out, but I think you've proven that just coping isn't enough. You can function as a recovering sex addict. You can avoid sleeping with every cute guy you see. But that's not enough, is it? It'll keep you from making the same mistake you made with Mark Howard. It'll keep me from making the same mistake I made with Gabriel Anderson. But in the end, we'll both still feel miserable because..." His thoughts obviously stalled. He kept embracing her, but now Peter seemed stuck. This strong, handsome man couldn't finish this thought. He began shaking his head in frustration while holding onto Mary, as if to cling to it.

However, Mary tried to pick up where he left off. She found herself cradling his unshaven face and watching her reflection in his eyes. In that reflection, she saw what he was unable to put into words.

"We didn't confront the *emptiness*," Mary finally said. "We never tried to figure out what it was that made us feel so empty in the first place."

"Wow. Could it really be that simple?" Peter said.

"It sure doesn't sound simple."

"Maybe we're just making it difficult. Maybe we already know the source of that void. We just never had a reason to confront it when our addictions ruled our lives."

"Still seems pretty hard," Mary said.

"Does it have to be? What if we just followed our instincts?"

"Correct me if I'm wrong, but aren't those the same instincts that made us sex addicts in the first place?"

"You're only half-wrong," Peter said. "I think we followed those instincts down one path—one we only *thought* was right because we'd never tried anything else."

"And now you want to try it? At a time when we're both so utterly broken?" Mary asked, already tempted to follow his words.

"Why not? Maybe that makes this the best possible time

to try a new path…for both of us."

As he said these words, Mary felt those very instincts guide her in a whole new way. Peter drew closer to her as his embrace tightened. Mary caressed his face. Nothing about it made sense. Her brain urged her to stop and think, but another more powerful feeling urged her to keep going.

Mary smelled his breath and his distinctly masculine musk. It was intoxicating, sending her into a daze where she could no longer rationalize her actions. She had been in such a state before around attractive men, but this time felt different. It wasn't the same temptation that she had experienced before. It was something much deeper. Whatever it was, it led to an inevitable conclusion.

In an instant that stopped time, he leaned down to her and initiated an intimate kiss. The feelings that followed were overwhelming.

Mary had kissed many men before, but it had never felt like *this*. A strange shiver shot through her body. Her legs became weak while her arms became stronger, allowing her to embrace him even more tightly. He pulled her closer, allowing her to feel the full warmth of his body.

Many sensations flowed through her. Some were familiar. Others were entirely new. She felt arousal of the most basic kind, including that of the sensual variety that she knew so well. However, there was another breadth of sensation that came with it. Like reaching into a well of untapped potential, something else began to emerge. The more Mary tasted his lips, the more she wanted to embrace the feelings they evoked.

The moment left Mary locked in a feeling from which she could not escape. Then, an unexpected distraction jarred them from this feeling in the form of thunder.

"The fuck?" gasped Peter, abruptly ending the kiss and looking up.

For a moment, Mary thought divine forces had conspired against them. She was prepared to grab Peter by the face and pull him back into more passionate gestures. Then another round of thunder rocked them, this time even louder than before. That was when she looked up and saw exactly what Peter had seen.

"Um...when the hell did *this* happen?"

"I don't know, but it looks like Hartman County's record drought is about to end," Peter said.

"And we were *so* caught up in each other that we didn't notice?"

"Apparently," he replied.

It *had* to be a fluke, but Mary's own eyes confirmed it. Somehow, between the time when they'd started talking and the moment they'd kissed, it had gone from partly cloudy to overcast and from overcast to a full-blown thunderstorm. She didn't remember it getting cloudy or feeling the wind pick up. It showed just how engrossed she had been in Peter.

Fluke or not, Mary still tried to shake off the distraction, hoping to salvage what remained of this moment. Then rain started falling, and it wasn't a drizzle.

"This...could just be a quick shower," Mary said hopefully.

The sky must have heard her because it responded with a burst of lightning, followed by more thunder.

"You were saying?" Peter said in amusement.

"Come on! What we were doing was *important*, Mary said. "I don't care if this is a fucking tornado. We can't just leave it here."

"I don't want to, either," he said, "and we won't."

She wasn't sure what he meant by that, but she could tell that the firefighter in Peter was assessing this like any other emergency situation. He looked at her then back at the sky. Then, he turned to her again.

"My apartment's not far from here. If we hurry, we can get there before the worst of it hits," Peter said.

"That sounds *somewhat* logical," Mary said nervously.

"Except..." he said.

"That's skipping a few steps. What we just did... We're

living dangerously here, Peter. We're *still* a couple of recovering sex addicts, last I checked. Put us together alone in an apartment and what do you think will happen?"

The circumstances were impossible to ignore. They would be breaking every spoken and unspoken rule they'd agreed on. She and Peter couldn't put themselves in a situation where the temptation would be too great. However, after what they'd just done, they seemed past that point already.

"I know what I'm asking sounds like a bad idea. Us being soaking wet probably doesn't help," Peter said.

"Doesn't help that I dressed light today, either," Mary said, still shivering in the pouring rain.

"But maybe this is a sign. Maybe this is nature's way of telling us we need to be bolder. I'll still leave it up to you. Just know that I've done a lot of things in my life that only felt right at the time. This—whatever this might be—I *know* it's right."

He sounded so certain, but Mary remained conflicted. Heavier rain and another burst of thunder added urgency to her decision. It started coming down so hard that most of her clothes were already soaked. A sharp gust of wind followed, sending a cold shiver through her body. It was as if fate itself wanted her to follow Peter.

Sister Angela wouldn't approve. Nobody who understood sex addiction would approve, either. However, with the sensations of the kiss still fresh in Mary's mind, she saw the potential for something greater. It might save her soul or break her spirit, but she would never find out if she kept running. Having done enough of that, she made her decision.

"Okay. Let's go!" Mary said, her shivering hiding her reservations. "Take me to your apartment, but let's at least *try* to minimize the temptation."

"Understood," Peter said with a smile. "I can't make any promises, though."

"Me, neither. I'm not sure I want to."

Before either of them could have second thoughts, Peter

led her away from the picnic table and toward the parking lot. Mary clung to his arm and stayed close, still feeling the warmth that she had only gotten a taste of. It gave her even more incentive to see things through.

The rain fell harder and the wind picked up. This was the kind of storm that wasn't just going to pass them by. They were going to have to hunker down and wait it out, giving them plenty of time to finish what they'd started. Mary still had no idea where it would lead, but she was tempted to find out, and for once, she felt tempted for all the right reasons.

Chapter Thirteen

"It's official. The universe is fucking with us," groaned Mary, now cold and shivering from running through the storm.

"I don't know what to tell you *or* the universe," Peter said, who was just as soaked. "My landlord did mention something yesterday about some utility work in the basement. Guess he didn't plan on the weather, either."

"Does that mean the power won't be coming back on anytime soon?"

"It…might be a while," Peter said in a less-than-optimistic tone.

Mary muttered a string of curses under her breath as she hugged her shoulders to stop the shivering. They'd arrived at Peter's apartment building just as the storm had gotten really bad. It was like a miniature hurricane. Heavy rain and high winds hammered the area that had only known drought for months. It had caught everyone off-guard, adding even more complications to the emotionally tense predicament.

Shortly after they'd made it into the building, the power had gone out. That meant they couldn't distract themselves with movies or TV. She and Peter would now be in a darkened apartment, soaking wet and with little to do.

It felt like one of those scenarios that could turn into a horror movie or a porno. Mary could already hear Sister Angela's voice urging her to leave, but she promised herself she would see this through. Already, it felt like her resolve was being tested.

"I'll get some towels," Peter said after closing the door

behind them. "Just make yourself comfortable...relatively speaking."

"I'll try, but I'm in the apartment of a guy I just kissed. That's going to be tricky," Mary reminded him.

"Yeah. I imagine it would be," he replied awkwardly.

"Did you expect the power to go out?"

"No, but I think it's best we temper our expectations from here on out."

Mary rolled her eyes and hugged her shoulders, still shivering from the wet cold. While Peter went to retrieve the towels, she made her way into the apartment.

Overall, it was a fairly decent place. It looked like it was a one-bedroom, one-bathroom apartment with a gas fireplace and an average-sized living room. She could tell he had just moved in. There were still boxes stacked along the walls near the fireplace. The only pieces of furniture he had were a small sofa with an end table and a TV stand.

There were no pictures or décor on the walls, nothing that would indicate he had once been a womanizing pussy hound. If he had anything he could've used to impress a woman, he'd obviously left it behind in LA. For someone trying to get away from the reckless life he'd once lived, it seemed fitting.

Mary ended sitting down on the sofa. With the power out and nothing else raising her suspicions, she gazed through of the window overlooking town. Since the apartment was several floors up, she had a nice view of Hartman County's urban areas. The view revealed that the universe wasn't picking only on them.

The street lights and windows for several blocks were dark, indicating that the power outage went beyond this building. It also revealed the size and scope of the storm. If the darkness of the clouds was any indication, the storm would last for quite a while. That meant she was stuck here for the time being

After the gravity of her predicament set in, Mary contemplated what would happen next. She thought back to the kiss that the storm had interrupted. She could still taste Peter's lips on hers, still recall the way his arms felt around her. In her shivering state, Mary really longed for that warmth right about now. At the same time, she tried to scrutinize all the feelings that kiss had evoked in her.

What are you doing here? What do you want from this man? she asked herself.

As she watched the rain fall, Mary went over the possibilities. The most obvious also happened to be dangerous. Maybe those feelings were the product of repressed sexual urges. It made some sense, as evidenced by her recent masturbation habits. The whole ordeal could just be the byproduct of a sex-addicted woman who just *really* wanted to have sex again. If that was the case, then Mary might as well brave the storm, because she would only hurt herself and Peter by giving in.

She refused to accept the possibility. There had been something else in that kiss. Those lustful inclinations were present, but there were more powerful feelings at work. It couldn't be that she was falling in love with the guy. Love didn't work that way. Even if it did, it still wouldn't be sufficient.

That kiss had just been the culmination of many feelings. All those things they'd talked about earlier, from her descent into addiction to her struggles to recover, had acted as a spark of sorts. Mary had never been so open and honest with someone before. Perhaps talking about those experiences had revealed something she had missed in her previous efforts to deal with her problems. It was the least-obvious possibility, but one that offered the most tantalizing outcomes.

"Hey. Sorry I took so long," Peter said, breaking her train of thought as he entered the room. "I had to sift through a few boxes."

"That's okay. I didn't expect you to be that organized," Mary said. "It never was your style."

"You're not still mad at me for losing your biology

textbook, are you?" Peter asked as he tossed her a towel.

"You mean the one from sixth grade? The one that got me a week of detention?" teased Mary. "Now that you mention it, I *am* still mad."

"Sorry. I can't get that week back for you, but I can get you some coffee if the gas is still working."

"I guess it'll have to do," she said with mild annoyance. "We're still not even, though."

They both laughed, which helped ease the tension. They might have been a couple of recovering sex addicts in a very awkward situation, but neither she nor Peter had forgotten that they had once been friends. Mary took comfort in that friendship, even as she contemplated the more intimate possibilities.

As Peter walked to the kitchen, Mary stood and dried herself off with the towel. She then looked over and watched the handsome man from her youth work the stove.

He still wore the same pants as earlier, but he'd changed his shirt. If he had been trying to seduce her, he probably would've just strutted out in his underwear and let her hormones do the rest. That clearly wasn't his agenda, though. He'd kept those feelings in check, much to her relief.

However, they must still be affecting him. He fumbled around with the stove, struggling to get one of the panels lit. He seemed every bit as distracted as she was, appearing way too tense. Mary laughed to herself, wondering if he was contemplating the same intimate possibilities. Distractions aside, Peter finally got the stove going.

"Ah! There we go," Peter said with a sigh of relief. "The gas is still working, so we won't freeze or starve."

"You make it sound like we're snowed in or something," Mary said.

"I know. Sorry if I sound paranoid. I guess I just got too comfortable in the predictable Southern California weather."

As he said that, he spilled some of the instant coffee

powder onto his kitchen table. Mary snickered, much to his chagrin. For a well-conditioned firefighter, he was pretty clumsy and she had a good idea why.

"You sure don't look comfortable, but I'm guessing that's not because of the weather."

"Speak for yourself, Mary. You're still giving me that look," retorted Peter smugly.

"What look? You think I'm going to fall into the same trap as every other girl you've lured into your apartment?" teased Mary.

"You always were a step ahead of me. I doubt any of my tricks would work on you, so I'll save myself the trouble."

"You better. I came here for a reason, remember? I still don't know the extent of that reason, but I'm determined to find out," she said in a more serious tone.

"So am I," Peter said.

He sounded every bit as serious. It convinced Mary that he was committed to finishing what they'd started. It might not mean sharing another kiss, but she tried not to make too many assumptions.

As she watched Peter make the coffee, she pondered their next step. How exactly could they pick up where they'd left off? One moment they had been kissing and the next moment they had found themselves in the middle of a storm. Before that, it had felt like she and Peter were on the brink of a profound realization. In hearing the story of how her addiction had broken her, he'd seen something that she hadn't, and now Mary was determined to see it, too.

Once he'd finished making the coffee, he walked over to the living room and handed her a cup. With a hot beverage in hand, Mary sat back down on the couch with the damp towel draped around her neck. He didn't sit down with her, though. As she drank to warm herself, Peter activated the gas fireplace. He managed to get it going without incident, providing them with much-needed light and heat.

In any other circumstance, this would've been a romantic, sensual mood. Instead, a great deal of tension lingered, only some of which was sexual.

"So...how do you want to handle this?" Mary asked.

"I don't know. I didn't think that far ahead when I invited you here," admitted Peter.

"And for once, you can't blame your penis. How sad is that?" Mary said.

"Very, but if we're going to finish what we started, then we need to stay serious."

"I am being serious. It is kind of pathetic when you think about it...us ending up here and our sexual urges having little to do with it. That says to me that we're too used to things being simple, getting just intimate enough to get laid and not much else beyond that."

"When you put it like that, it sounds more tragic than pathetic," Peter said.

"It works both ways. It might be why I kissed you and didn't know what the hell to make of it. I guess if we're really going to take this head on, let's start with that kiss, because I'd like to know what went into it."

"That makes two of us."

They were officially on the same page now. Peter looked just as conflicted about the kiss as she was. Mary also noticed that he remained near the fireplace, still keeping his distance, while she sat on the sofa.

He wouldn't say it, but she could tell he was reluctant to get close in a way that would risk greater temptation. It wasn't just sexual temptation, either. Another kiss might just add to the confusion. Before they could be that bold, they needed to confront this.

"That kiss was... Well, it was...nice," Peter said with a slight smile.

"No argument here. It was definitely something," Mary said with a smile of her own. "Would it be just as sad if I told you that you're the first person I've kissed in a year?"

"Not necessarily," Peter said. "A kiss is usually an effect, not a cause. So why don't we focus on the stuff that came before it?"

"Good idea, but you're the one who kissed me, so I'm not sure I can say much."

"You're right. I am the one who triggered it. You just accepted it. That may not sound like much, but it's worth thinking about."

"Why do you say that?" Mary asked.

"Because when I was doing my reckless man-whoring, I took the exact opposite approach. I *never* instigated a kiss. I just charmed the woman until she made the first move."

"You think that matters?"

"Yeah, I think it matters a lot," Peter said. As he sipped his coffee, he began pacing around his living room. It shouldn't have been a big deal, him making the first move. Most men who had significant dating experience wouldn't have batted an eye. The fact he found it so jarring made it worth scrutinizing.

"But why does it matter?" he muttered under his breath. "It shouldn't, but—"

"It does matter. And it matters for a reason," Mary said, following his train of thought. "And a good reason that's worth knowing."

That continued to bother them both. While Peter paced, Mary thought about it as well. It had been almost as jarring, a man being so direct with her. It had flipped the script she usually followed when hooking up with a man. She'd had to be the one doing the seducing, from that first interested gaze to the moment clothes started coming off. That hadn't happened this time. Instead, Peter had made the first move and she'd just accepted it.

Something about that stuck with her. Mary closed her eyes and relived that moment while the memory was still fresh. In doing so, she experienced some of those feelings again. This time, they weren't nearly as overwhelming. This allowed her to process them, which led to a few realizations.

"We've kissed people before. I've kissed men much harder than I kissed you. I'm sure you've kissed women just as much…and not always on the lips," Mary said

"I'd rather not speak to *that,* so I'll just resist the urge to comment," Peter said, still pacing. "Are you going somewhere with this, Mary?"

"Bear with me, Peter, because I don't think it was the intensity of that kiss that made it feel so different. I think it was the setup. Based on what you told me about your womanizing ways, it went like this... You got her intrigued, you got her in the mood then—once the blood started flowing in the right directions—you let her instincts do the rest. You let her set the pace and the program. Am I accurate so far?"

"In the most basic sort of way? Yeah, I'd say so," affirmed Peter.

"I did something similar, but in *reverse,*" continued Mary. "I got the guy intrigued, I got him aroused, then once we agreed to do the deed, *I* took the initiative. I made sure *I* controlled the situation, from foreplay to climax to afterglow. That means if we didn't know each other and just randomly hooked up, our methods would've complemented each other perfectly."

"I'd say that's accurate, too. You think that's why it felt strange? It was just so different?"

"I don't think so. Novelty alone only goes so far, especially for a couple of sex addicts. I think there was something deeper at work."

"Something else? Like what?"

Peter stopped pacing and leaned on the wall near the fireplace. Mary took another sip of her coffee, still recalling that kiss. Her gaze shifted toward the window, where the storm continued to escalate.

Heavy rains kept pouring amid frequent thunder and lightning. It was a complete reversal of the hot, dry conditions that had sent Hartman County into a record drought. In a sense, it mirrored her and Peter's experience perfectly.

"Sister Angela once said that we become addicted to things because we use them to fill a hole in our souls. She also said something about filling that hole with something positive. In her case, she filled it with Jesus. I guess that works for her, but I also think she's missing the bigger picture," Mary said.

"Like what created that hole in the first place," surmised Peter.

"Exactly!" she said. "We both have that hole in us, to some extent. It might not be the same, but we've used the same tactics to fill it."

"With sex?"

"Not just sex—a very *particular* approach to sex. We needed to do it a certain way. We needed to follow a certain path—one that became a coping skill of sorts."

"If it was a coping skill, it wasn't a very good one. It still messed us up big time," Peter said.

"Very true, but that's still not the full story," Mary said. "We could've used other unhealthy methods to cope—pot, cocaine, junk food. Hell, we had options. It still ended up being sex."

"How much does the method really matter?"

"I think it matters more than we think. If it didn't, then that kiss wouldn't have felt so overwhelming. This leads me to believe there's a reason we got addicted to sex, and maybe it has something to do with the way we approached it."

Peter fell silent, drinking the rest of his coffee and giving her the look he only gave when he was really stuck on something. Mary finished hers and set the cup aside. She stopped reliving the moment of the kiss in her mind and turned back toward the man standing before her.

She had talked before about the reasons sex had become her addiction of choice. In fact, Mary had talked about it to the point of frustration with Sister Angela during her first three months in the program. Before their earlier talk, the nun had often focused on the treatment rather than the cause, which might be why her efforts had never felt sufficient. This told Mary that there was something important they both had overlooked and kissing Peter had helped expose it.

"When you kissed me, you took a *different* approach," Mary said. "You were in a position to get something you wanted, but you took another path to get it."

"That implies my only intent was to get you into bed with me. That's *not* what I wanted, Mary," Peter said.

"So...what? You're not attracted to me? You don't find me sexy?"

"Don't do that, Mary. This isn't a game."

"I wasn't trying to make it a game," she continued. "It's a serious factor to consider. There's definitely *some* attraction we're avoiding. I think we felt it that first night we met. If we didn't, you wouldn't have run off on me."

Peter looked uncomfortable again. He didn't flat-out admit that he was attracted to her, but he didn't have to. Mary could see the signs.

She hadn't bothered avoiding it. Her attraction to him had become abundantly clear, as her recent masturbation habits had demonstrated. Without revealing those intimate details, she gave him a reassuring smile to ease the tension. It helped somewhat, but it also helped make her point.

"It's okay. It doesn't have to be weird. You're an attractive guy. I'm an attractive girl. We've already got a history. There's bound to be some mutual interest involved," Mary said.

"Attraction, lust, love, whatever you want to call it... It's a few steps beyond weird," Peter said awkwardly.

"Maybe that's a sign that there's something *right* about it. When we kissed—whatever method we used—it still felt *right*. In fact, it felt so right that I'm starting to think the solution is more obvious than we're willing to admit."

"Solution? Solution to what?"

"I'm not sure. I'm just thinking out loud here," admitted Mary. "All I know is that when I kissed you, I felt something that filled that emptiness inside me—something that I'm just now starting to understand."

The mood between her and Peter shifted. The emotions she'd felt at that moment became secondary. The forces that evoked those emotions took priority.

Mary could tell he was reliving the kiss in his mind, trying to understand it as she did. The way he looked at her made the extent of those emotions clear. It was enough to make Mary feel awkward, but it didn't keep her from smiling.

"It's strange. The more I think about it, the less weird it seems," Peter said. "Maybe that's another sign."

"I don't know about you, but I'm tired of just identifying the signs. I'm more interested in what they're saying," Mary said.

"So, what are they saying? Is it really just a matter of needing someone you want to both love *and* fuck?"

"You think a solution to something like this could be that simple?"

"It would be nice if it were. It would make a terrible romantic comedy, but it wouldn't be completely outrageous," Peter said. "We both admitted to keeping things casual when exercising our addiction. I remember resisting the urge to seek any emotional entanglement with someone. This might be the resistance of those urges catching up with me."

"If that's the case, then the kiss would've been downright hollow," Mary said. "That would make all those feelings as genuine as the ones we'd get from a run-of-the-mill one-night stand."

"Which is exactly why I guess that's not the case," Peter said. "You said you felt something that actually filled the void. Just releasing pent-up desires wouldn't do that. It would only replace one kind of emptiness with another."

"Makes sense," shrugged Mary.

"So then, it's not just that we crave a connection with someone that involves something other than swapping bodily fluids," continued Peter. "It's more that we never learned how to make it in the first place. We only knew one way to connect, but that way only went so far. Then, today, we tried a new way and something else came from it — something amazing."

As he said the words, he finally smiled back at her. It made Mary feel awkward in a way she hadn't since her teen years. It was unfamiliar, but not uncomfortable.

With the tension fading rapidly, Peter finally sat down on the sofa next to her. She was tempted to move in closer and slip into his arms, but she held back. A part of her wanted to tempt him as she had tempted many men, but she didn't want to do that. In the end, Mary didn't have to.

For a brief moment, Peter just sat there and gave her an affectionate gaze. The way he looked at her made her feel something that went beyond attraction. It couldn't just be lust. It couldn't just be love, either. This had to be something *more*. He clearly felt it, as well, and wanted more of it, just as she did.

"But as amazing as it was, it was still...*incomplete*," Peter said.

"Which wasn't our fault, mind you," reminded Mary, just as another round of thunder hit.

"Well, we're indoors now — alone, out of sight and with exceedingly few distractions. We've already told our respective stories. We've been brutally honest with each other."

"Maybe even too brutal," added Mary.

"Be that as it may, there's not much left to say. If we wanted, we could try to complete the feeling."

"I thought that was the main reason for inviting me to your apartment...and all the implications that come with it."

"It is. So, I guess the only thing stopping us now is... Do we even know?"

That was the burning question. Before she dared to evoke any more intense feelings with Peter, she had to determine how to confront all this.

That first kiss between them had just happened. It had been a culmination of instinct, and she couldn't rely on that again. In fact, relying on instinct was a big part of what had led her and Peter into their current predicament. To truly break the cycle that had fueled their sexual addiction, they needed to do something much bolder.

Mary opened her mouth to offer an answer, but nothing came out. Her mind went blank. Her train of thought had hit a dead end. Doing something bold had never scared Mary before. No woman ever had ever become a successful model or an unapologetic slut by being shy. However, something like this required a different kind of boldness.

Her silence seemed to disappoint Peter. He must have been at just as much a loss. Letting out an exasperated sigh, he shook his head and turned back toward the fire in his fireplace.

"Sorry," he said. "I was kind of hoping *you* had the answer, because this is where my expertise ends."

"I'm as disappointed as you. I'm usually pretty good at coming up with something…even if it is crazy," Mary said.

"You always were full of crazy ideas as a kid," Peter said. "For this, we may need something extra weird."

He remained fixated on the fire. Mary tried to encourage him, reaching over and placing a hand on his leg. It didn't have the effect she'd hoped for, but it should remind him that they were in this together—however right or wrong it ended up being.

While Peter stared distantly into the fire, Mary decided not to strain herself more than she already had. She slumped in her seat, resting her head on the back of the sofa. For a moment, she just watched the fire with Peter. It offered a warm, soothing ambience in the midst of a raging storm. It helped her relax, but it didn't give her any ideas.

As they sat in silence, Mary turned toward the window again and watched the storm outside rage on. The pouring rain pounded the windows. The wind and the thunder echoed from the sky. It was eerily beautiful, but that might have been a byproduct of the drought. It had been so long since Hartman County had seen any rain that a storm like this was a major spectacle.

Then, as Mary admired this sight, an idea came to her. She became more alert, as though she had just received an urgent message. She rose from the sofa, getting Peter's attention in the process, while she remained fixated on the raging storm outside.

"What is it, Mary? Is something wrong?" Peter asked.

He sounded worried but intrigued. The idea that had just popped into Mary's head was *beyond* crazy. For a moment, she tried convincing herself to forget it. She failed. In doing so, Mary only convinced herself that the idea was worth trying.

Now, standing in the middle of the living room, Mary turned back toward Peter. The idea might have been nuts, but it made too much sense. All the complications that had driven her into her sexual addiction took on a new context. Her mind began to race again, so much so that a smile formed on her face. In a moment that might define her fate and Peter's, Mary made a bold yet very unusual choice.

"Mary?" Peter said with growing curiosity.

"Let's have sex," Mary proclaimed with more enthusiasm than she'd intended. "Right here. Right now. Let's do it. Let's have sex!"

Chapter Fourteen

The next few moments tested Mary's ability to contain herself. She'd had a feeling she would get a reaction from Peter as soon as she proposed her idea. She just hadn't expected it to be so funny.

"I, uh... How did you...? What?" he exclaimed in bewilderment.

"You heard me. You know what I said. I'll say it again really slowly, just in case you didn't hear me right. Let's... have...sex," Mary said in a tone that left no room for ambiguity.

Peter had a look on his face that reminded her of a child who'd just seen an R-rated movie for the first time. Oddly enough, she remembered him making a similar face when they'd raided her brothers' porno stash when they were kids. For a man who carried himself with such strength, it was pretty hilarious.

His reaction aside, Mary remained dead serious. After saying it out loud, she suppressed any lingering doubts. For something like this to work, she couldn't have reservations.

"Um...I'm *still* going to need some context here," Peter said, gathering his composure just enough to form coherent sentences.

"I know. I just needed to gauge your reaction first," Mary said.

"I'd say you've got it. I'm pretty sure I've made an ass of myself already, so can you help me make sense of this?"

He sounded overwhelmed, having been caught completely off-guard. Mary held up her hands, encouraging him to settle down. He was probably making all sorts of assumptions, most of which weren't nearly as crazy as what Mary had in mind.

"Bear with me here," Mary said, still dead serious. "We've established a few hard facts. First and foremost, the way we kissed each other was different from all the other times we've kissed someone. With me so far?"

"I want to say yes, but doing so means I admit to having that urge," Peter said, being careful with his words.

"Are you going to tell me you haven't?" Mary asked with a raised eyebrow.

"I'll...let my erratic body language answer that."

"Fair enough," she said. "Now look at that kiss again. You said it yourself. You took the exact opposite approach. Not just a different approach — the exact opposite. We even agreed that meant something. Still with me?"

"Yeah...for the most part."

"And if it did mean something, then maybe we should take it even further. We've felt what happens when we flip the script on a kiss. Now, I want to see what happens when we do the same with sex."

"Sex? As in the very thing we're addicted to?" Peter said.

"Exactly!" affirmed Mary.

He remained baffled, and rightfully so. A kiss was one thing, but sex added a few complexities, to say the least. Lucky for him, Mary had already formulated a plan.

"It goes like this. You take the initiative in the sex. More importantly, though, you keep it. From foreplay to climax, *you* set the tone, the action and everything in between. In turn, I'll accept it. I'll trust you to do what needs to be done to ensure we're both satisfied."

"By initiative, you mean..." Peter said, still probing for details.

"I mean most of what you think I mean. You tell me what to do. You tell me how we're going to do it. It may mean me sucking your dick. It may mean you nibbling my ear, pinching my nipples or slapping my ass. I don't know. *You're* in charge. I'm just going to be a good girl and listen."

"So...you want me to *dominate* you?"

"No, it's not like that," Mary said, rolling her eyes. "I'm not talking full-blown BDSM here. This isn't about you dominating a woman or me being dominated by a man. This is about us doing something we've done before in a completely opposite way—a way that, for some reason, we've avoided. Maybe a part of that reason has to do with why all the sex we've had before left us feeling so empty."

It still sounded crazy, especially when she said it out loud, but Peter seemed to pick up on her line of thinking. He might be entertaining thoughts on how he would go about it, which definitely had appeal on some levels. Even so, Mary could tell he was hesitant.

She looked back briefly toward the window, the storm outside still raging. The spectacle had helped inspire the idea. As Mary watched the rain fall, she recalled the details of that inspiration.

"As sexual a woman as I am, I've been exceedingly uptight in my approach to sex," Mary said. "I use only one tool in a very specific way to fulfill my desires. I'm always the one to set the tone—always having to control the situation. It's like trying to fix a watch with a hammer. At some point, you need another tool to get the job done."

"And I did the same thing, albeit with a different tool," Peter said, following her logic. "I had to cede control to the woman to be the lover I thought *she* wanted me to be, but I was never the lover *I* wanted to be."

"In other words, we've only ever run half the race—seen only one side of a coin. In the same way too many sunny days can cause a drought, we've ignored other parts of our desires. We created that void that we've tried to fill in all the wrong ways. We created the cycle that turned our desires into full-blown addictions."

"So, to end that cycle, we should listen to those other desires. But what if that only leads to another cycle? One where we just crave a different kind of sex?"

"That's a distinct possibility," admitted Mary. "That

would tell us that our addictions go way beyond sex. I'm talking about the kind of addiction where wires get crossed and medications are needed."

That was a scary thought and one Sister Angela had warned every addict about at their first CHAOP meeting. Some forms of addiction were genuinely clinical, requiring both therapy and medicine. However, these were among the more severe cases. This didn't feel to Mary like one of them. It felt like something that was more personal than medical.

"I'm not ready to accept I'm in that kind of trouble just yet. I don't think you are, either," Mary said.

"We're still risking it, though," Peter said.

"We've already taken plenty of risks over these past few weeks. This one is definitely the biggest to date, but it might give us the biggest reward."

"How big?" he asked.

"One that will reveal whether this is just a relapse...or something far more meaningful," Mary said.

Another round of thunder echoed from the raging storm outside, as if nature itself was telling them the importance of the moment. Mary had made her decision. Still standing in the center of the living room, she shifted her gaze back to Peter, who had yet to make his choice.

There was no more shock or confusion. He now seemed to be giving her idea serious thought. It had to appeal to him on some level, if only as an opportunity to have sex with another beautiful woman.

However, she still remembered how he'd pushed her away that night they'd reconnected. Mary didn't doubt that Peter might do it again. He had just moved back to Hartman County, just begun his treatment for sex addiction. This could either derail that effort completely or spare him the year of misery Mary had endured.

She couldn't tell which way he was leaning. Usually, whenever Mary offered a man sex, his reaction was pretty predictable. This was uncharted territory, which only proved that her idea had merit.

For once, a sexual situation was completely out of her hands. For all she knew, Peter might decide to kick her out and make her wait out the storm in the hallway. She braced herself for whatever came, hoping that he would make the right decision for the right reasons.

The air grew tense. Peter remained conflicted. He just kept staring at her, as if he were looking for signs. Finally, his demeanor shifted. A smile crept across his face as he made his choice.

"Okay," Peter said with as much certainty as Mary had shown earlier.

"Okay?" Mary asked.

"Yes. Let's do this. Let's have sex. Let's see what comes of it."

"Great," Mary said with a profound sense of relief.

The hard part was officially over. She and Peter were on the same page. Now, it was time to see just how much more difficult this would get.

"So...do you need a moment? Do you need to set the mood or get into character?" Mary asked.

"No. That would defeat the purpose. I'm ready when you're ready," Peter said.

There was no going back now. Mary was going to have sex with this man. She had no idea what it would do to her, to Peter or to their friendship. It would either be a major relapse for a couple of hardened sex addicts or the start of something truly profound.

Chapter Fifteen

"All right, Peter Rogers, I am putty in your hands," proclaimed Mary. "Tell me what you want me to do."

These words felt so strange coming out of her mouth, her completely yielding to the whims of a man she had seduced. She was so used to making the first move, jumping a man's bones and letting her wild lust do the rest. This time, her legs trembled with a mix of fear and excitement, not knowing what he would ask of her.

Peter appeared just as overwhelmed. For all the women he'd slept with, she knew none of them had offered him something like this. She could tell his imagination was running faster than his brain could process. Whatever crazy plan he had in mind, Mary intended to follow it.

"Take your clothes off," he ordered her.

"Okay," replied Mary. "Want me to do a striptease or something?"

"I don't care how you do it. Just take your clothes off — shirt, pants, shoes, socks — *everything*."

He spoke with an assertiveness she had never heard from him. It was pretty jarring, but in a good way. He was stepping into uncharted territory, and it clearly excited him. Mary prepared to enter it with him.

In accordance with Peter's whims, she began to strip. She casually grasped the hem of her shirt and slid it over her head, revealing the black bra she was wearing. Then, Mary pushed down the straps of her bra and unhooked the clap in the center, letting it fall from her body. As soon as her ample breasts were fully exposed, she got a clear reaction from Peter.

"Nice," he said in a barely audible voice.

Mary smiled at his reaction. He had probably seen many pairs of big breasts. Having lived in Los Angeles, he had probably seen some much bigger and rounder than hers. But he was clearly getting turned on, and the way he did so aroused Mary, as well.

She let him admire her rack for a brief moment. He probably didn't even register when she resumed stripping. Still facing him, Mary undid the button of the black denim pants she had worn. She began pulling them down her thighs, revealing her matching black panties. Then, following a whim, she turned around and made it into a striptease of sorts.

In her head, Mary heard her favorite dance music from the clubs back in Miami. Following the beat, she swayed her hips sensually as she pulled the tight pants down to her ankles.

As she leaned over to remove her shoes and socks, she made sure Peter had a perfect view of her ass. A year ago, she probably would've been wearing an obscenely revealing thong. It didn't matter, though. Even with a pair of simple black panties that she'd bought on sale at a department store, she tried to make it look sexy.

"Nice," Peter said again, his voice barely above a whisper.

His reaction turned Mary on even more. She hadn't planned this. She hadn't thought about it. She'd just done it because he'd told her to. For once, she didn't have to put all her energy into seducing him. She could just be sexy on her own. There was something liberating about that.

Upon stepping out of her shoes and pants, only her black panties remained. Mary let Peter admire her butt a little longer before turning around again. She continued swaying her hips, putting on a show for him. She even teased him a little, pretending to take off her panties and exposing just bits and pieces of her covered flesh. While he seemed to enjoy her sensual display, he clearly wanted more.

"I said *everything*, remember?" Peter said in the same

commanding voice as when they'd started.

Mary got the message. He didn't want to be teased. He just wanted her naked. With that in mind, she dispensed with the theatrics and removed her panties. She still did it slowly, retaining some of the mood.

Now completely naked, Mary just stood in the center of the living room. His gaze drifted up and down her body, scrutinizing her every feature. He gave special attention to her breasts, her hips, her legs and the sexy part between them.

Warmth flushed through Mary. It felt kind of strange, being this vulnerable. There was also something exciting about it, because she had no idea what Peter would ask of her next.

"You look...beautiful," he said distantly.

"Thank you, but I had a feeling you already felt that way about my body," Mary said. "Remember, you're the one in control here. *You* have the leverage. You can have even more if you want, but I'm not going to make suggestions. You have to want it and take it."

She'd dared him to be bolder. She might have to double-dare him, because he still hesitated. Mary could tell he was very aroused by his breathing and the bulge in his jeans. Just doing what he'd asked — something as simple as taking her clothes off — had excited him to the point of seemingly being overwhelmed.

His breathing intensified as he drifted his gaze up and down her naked body. His mind must have been racing, musing over everything he could make her do for him. Finally, a devious grin formed on his face. He must have come up with a way to respond to her dare, making her both nervous and excited.

"Okay, then," Peter said in a strangely casual tone. "You just proved to me I'll need more than your permission to do what I want to do. I'll also need a little incentive."

Before Mary could even ask what that implied, he acted. That smile never waned as he got up from the sofa and gathered up her discarded clothes. Once in hand, he walked over to the sliding door that opened to his patio. Then, he casually tossed them into the pouring rain, leaving them crumpled up next to a deck table.

It was a surprising and unexpected exercise of his new authority. Initially, Mary was irritated. At least he'd left her purse alone, which contained her wallet and cell. Even so, his actions left her feeling even more naked, knowing that she didn't have anything to put back on.

She instinctively folded her arms over her breasts and shifted uncomfortably, but she didn't voice any complaints. She just watched Peter close the door, lock it and make his way back to the sofa where he sat down, showing a weird sense of accomplishment.

"There. Now we both have additional incentive," Peter said.

"Both of us?" questioned Mary.

"Yep," he said proudly. "I actually have more leverage. You said if I wanted it, I had to take it, so that's exactly what I did. Now, you can't just grab your clothes and run off if you change your mind — not unless you want to run naked through a major storm."

"I wasn't planning to, but I guess that's not a viable option anymore anyway."

"That's the point. You've had so many options. You took them. I had to work to get what I got with all the women I slept with. Now, it's going to be the other way around. You want your clothes back? You want me to throw them in the dryer or give you a blanket? You'll have to work for it. That's incentive for you."

It sounded so perverse in concept, making her work just to get her clothes back. At the same time, it was pretty damn pragmatic. It gave her more incentive to do as he said, but the impact went beyond that.

Just making her strip naked hadn't been enough. She sensed Peter had needed to assert his control over the situation to get to the next level. It must have been exhilarating because he had an intense focus in his eyes, hinting that he was done hesitating.

"Some incentive," Mary said, tensing at the notion.

"No need to be nervous. I won't exploit it unnecessarily. You can trust me on that," assured Peter.

"I'm already trusting you way more than I've trusted every other man who's seen me naked."

"And it shows. You're nervous, but excited. I can tell this is thrilling for you, ceding control to someone and trusting they'll use it responsibly. I guess you'll just have to trust that my feelings for you are strong enough to keep that in mind."

This man was asking a lot of her, but it also revealed something important. Peter Rogers wasn't just some random hot guy. He was an old friend who had become something more over the past few weeks.

Mary had let herself get emotionally entangled with him—something she had avoided with so many men for so long. The kiss they'd shared earlier had revealed some strong feelings between them. If she wanted to connect with him—and possibly evoke even more powerful emotions—she needed to truly trust Peter.

"So, what did you have in mind?" Mary asked, now no longer covering her breasts.

"It's nothing unreasonable, I promise. It might even be something you've done before...although you may not have done it sober," Peter said mischievously.

He stretched his limbs and relaxed somewhat, allowing himself to get more comfortable on the sofa. He was really in the spirit of things now. Still not knowing what he had planned, Mary awaited his next order.

"Give me a lap dance—a full-nude, full-contact lap dance," Peter said.

"Okay. I admit that's not as unreasonable as I expected," Mary said.

"So, you have done it before," he said.

"Once or twice—sober *and* not sober," she replied. "Are

there any special rules I should consider?"

"This isn't a club. My rules are different, but they're simple. Just start dancing. I'll tell you what to touch, when to touch it and how. Understand?"

"Perfectly," Mary said.

"Good. Now, since the power is out, I only have my phone. It's not a boom box at a club, but it's better than nothing."

"It'll do," she assured.

As Mary prepared herself, Peter retrieved his cell phone from his pocket then loaded the music he had on it. After selecting a few tracks, he set the phone down on the table next to the sofa and started the first song. It wasn't the kind of heavy, fast-paced music that often echoed from the clubs in Miami, but it would suffice.

Before the music even started, Mary had closed her eyes and lightly traced her hands up and down her naked body. The idea of giving a man a lap dance didn't make her too anxious. Mary had put on sexy shows for men before and those shows had included lap dances, both clothed and unclothed. However, those dances had always been on her terms. This would be different.

Since she would be playing by Peter's rules this time, Mary didn't overthink it. As soon as she heard music, she just began dancing. She swayed and swerved her upper body sensually, shaking her hips and playing with her breasts. With the sound of the rain falling outside, she established a sultry rhythm.

When she opened her eyes, she saw that Peter clearly approved of her approach. He paid special attention to her breasts and hips. It gave Mary incentive to be even sexier, moving her hips more rapidly and touching herself more seductively. It evoked a range of feelings that led to a special kind of arousal.

"Come in closer," Peter said, his voice echoing with heightened interest.

Mary did as he asked, strutting toward him like he was

some high roller at a strip club. When she reached the sofa, she kept on moving to the music, never straying from the rhythm. She resisted her inclination to tempt him. She'd wait to do what he asked. It was strange, her *not* taking the initiative as she had always done. That helped make it so meaningful...among other things.

"Lean over. Rub your boobs in my face," ordered Peter.

He sounded like a teenage boy's fantasy, so eager and immature. There was something oddly refreshing about that. Mary mirrored that sentiment as she complied with his request, playfully shoving his face between her ample breasts. She then shook her chest back and forth, allowing him to enjoy their warmth.

As she did so, Mary got on the couch and sat on his lap, her knees now resting at his sides. Still swaying to the beat of the music, she let her pelvis make contact with his. She could already feel a bulge in his pants from his growing manhood. She could even feel him breathing heavily between her breasts. This seemed to be exciting him in ways that were anything but immature.

"Big, soft and natural. You're very well-endowed, Mary," Peter said as he looked up from her cleavage. "Now turn around and start grinding against me. Let's see if your ass is just as endowed."

"Yes, sir, Mr. Rogers," Mary said in a seductive tone.

Slipping deeper into the spirit of the moment, Mary shifted her body so that she faced away from him. Now, her butt pressed right up against the bulge in his pants. Taking full advantage of the position, she playfully rocked and swayed, grinding her rump against the rough denim containing his hard cock. Peter reacted favorably, letting out a contented grunt as she put a little extra force into it.

"Yeah! Just like that," he told her.

Then, in an act that would've gotten him kicked out of a typical strip club, he grabbed her ass with both of his hands and gave it a firm squeeze. His strong grip sent shivers up and down Mary's body. It accelerated her growing need, creating a powerful heat in her core that was building rapidly.

The sensual energy was overwhelming. Mary kept following it, making a concerted effort to draw Peter into it with her. He seemed to embrace it as well. At one point, he maneuvered her so that she was bent over the couch arm with her hands on the floor, allowing her ass to dominate his view. He made good use of his leverage, rubbing and squeezing her butt as he pleased. He even gave it a few hard swats.

This startled Mary at first. He hadn't asked for permission. She hadn't demanded it of him, either. He'd just done it, following whims he'd told her he'd never dared follow before. The swats hadn't been too hard or too soft. They had been delivered with just the right amount of impact.

As he continued swatting, the heat building in Mary's core made one thing clear. This was a very different sexual experience from those that had fueled their addictions. Even though Peter was in a perfect position to exploit his control, he hadn't. That evoked a strange feeling in her, mixing basic sensual need with a more complex emotional response.

It felt like something she should've pursued years ago. Already, she was getting more out of this than she had any sexual experience in her recent memory. It kept growing in intensity and energy, leaving Mary wanting more.

"Such a nice ass," Peter said, giving it another swat.

"Thanks. I work hard on it," Mary said.

"It shows. It's enough to make a man crazy."

Showing increasing assertiveness, Peter grabbed her by the waist and pulled her back into an upright position. He reached around and gave her breasts a hard squeeze.

This triggered a sharp gasp from Mary, revealing the extent of her arousal. Her entire core trembled under the growing heat within her. Her heart rate spiked and she felt a light sweat forming on her naked skin. She could no longer keep dancing to the music. Her excitement made it too difficult, and Peter took notice.

"You're really getting turned on from this, aren't you?" he asked in a half-serious tone.

"I am," she replied.

"So am I. Guess that means we're doing something right, so let's keep doing it."

"And how do you want to go about that? You're still in charge, remember?"

"Oh, I remember," Peter said.

He proved his point by grabbing her waist again and turning her around so she faced him. He looked at her with such domineering authority. The way he held her and ran his hands over her naked body... It showed that he had fully embraced this mentality.

"Now, I want you to get on your knees, undo my pants and give me a blow job," he said assertively.

"Still keeping it nice and simple, eh?" Mary said.

"I wasn't finished. While you're sucking my dick, I want you to finger your pussy until you come. See if you can get off before me."

"Is that a challenge?"

"It can be," he said, "or you can just look at it as more incentive."

This man knew how to encourage a girl, likely a byproduct of motivating himself to be better. Mary didn't complain.

With a seductive smile, Mary went to work. The music was still playing, so she kept moving a bit, still treating it like a lap dance. She swayed her hips and torso, slithering her way down his body and trailing her hands down his chest. Peter leaned back on the couch, giving Mary room to work. Through the erotic movements, she slipped deeper into that sexy state of mind that she had avoided for over a year.

By the time she reached the floor, she was in the perfect mood for the task before her. Now on her knees between Peter's thighs, Mary had an up-close view of the bulge in his pants.

With no desire to make him wait longer than necessary, she undid his belt and unzipped his pants. Once loosened, Peter lifted his hips slightly so Mary could get the items off. She reached for the sides and gave a hard tug, pulling his jeans and boxers down to his knees to free his erect penis.

"Thanks. Those were getting uncomfortable," Peter said.

"I'll say. You've been holding out on me, Peter. You're also quite endowed," Mary said as she admired his erect cock.

"I'd say you're just being polite, but you're not the first woman to point that out."

"Then you know I'm being honest, so believe me when I say I'll give you the best blow job I've ever given."

Those were bold words from an admitted sex addict who had been giving blow jobs since high school. Mary doubted she had been the only woman who'd made Peter such a promise, but none of those women had been in a situation like this. It only motivated her.

"I'll hold you to that, Mary," Peter said with a grin. "Now, start sucking. Prove to me that you can keep your promise."

With focused determination, Mary went to work on Peter's cock. She used both hands at first, grasping the base of his shaft with one while fondling his balls with the other. He tensed under her grip, an instinctive reaction to a skilled touch. Then she gave his hard length a few good strokes to get more blood flowing. His cock throbbed in her hand, aching for more. She didn't wait for him to urge her.

She started by giving the head a messy kiss. Then she used her tongue to lick around the sensitive glans while continuing to massage his balls. His member throbbed even more. When she sensed he couldn't get any harder, Mary took the plunge, fully engulfing as much of him as her mouth would allow.

"Damn, Mary!" gasped Peter. "You're...you're good at this!"

Mary barely heard his praise. She was too focused on making this the best oral sex she had ever given. She went on by licking and sucking along his rigid penis. His endowment tested her gag reflex and her jaw muscles, but Mary made it a point to push herself. Slipping deeper into a sexual daze, she established a rhythm, bobbing her head up and down his member while slithering her tongue along his length.

"Ooh, that's it! Just like that! Use your tongue…just like *that!*" Peter said through labored breaths.

Mary opened her eyes to look up and see the blissful look on his face. She usually kept her eyes closed during oral sex. There was something satisfying about seeing a man she had genuine feelings for look so content. It only added to her motivation.

"Don't…don't forget…to touch yourself. Remember?" he managed to say.

His words forced Mary to intensify her focus. In her desire to make good on her promise, she'd forgotten about the other part of Peter's request. His not-so-subtle reminder triggered some overdue instincts.

Mary reached between her thighs and began touching herself. She wasn't gentle, either. She skipped the usual steps, plunging two fingers into the folds of her dripping vagina while using her thumb to massage her clit.

She'd managed to get pretty hot while giving Peter his lap dance, but she needed to fuel the growing feeling. He'd dared her to give herself an orgasm before he got his. Being a competitive person by nature, Mary had every intention of meeting that challenge.

Before long, she began fondling herself with the same rhythm as her oral teasing. Every time Mary plunged her lips down Peter's cock, she jammed her fingers into her pussy. It created a perfect feedback loop, sending shots of pleasure through her body as she did the same to Peter. Soon, they were both moaning in contentment, so much so that it drowned out the music still playing on his phone. At that point, he reached over and turned it off so there were no more distractions.

Now, the only noises that could be heard were Peter's deep grunts and Mary's sucking. They were familiar sounds and feelings. Mary had experienced them many times before, but not like this.

"Mary...do it harder! Suck me...*harder!*" urged Peter.

Mary complied. She slid her lips and tongue along his erect cock at a faster pace, adding more pressure to each movement. At the same time, Mary pumped her fingers into her vagina even faster. The escalating desire added a sense of urgency, if not outright desperation, in her pursuit of this growing feeling of intimacy.

The result was a rapid escalation of sensations. Mary felt it in the growing wetness that soaked her pussy. Her muscles began throbbing around her hand. She was getting close to an orgasm and it had happened much quicker than she'd expected.

"Mmm!" moaned Mary in a way that communicated her desires.

"Yeah...you want it, too. I can tell that you need it," Peter said through panting breaths.

Peter grabbed onto her head. Once he had a firm grip, he guided her up and down the length of his penis, establishing a more fervent rhythm. He also ran his fingers through her hair and lightly jerked his hips upward, adding more intensity to her ministrations. Mary adjusted herself accordingly, pushing her skills even further.

"Oh yeah! *That's* how I want it," Peter said. "I...I'm getting close. Just a little...bit more."

Mary looked up at him again briefly and saw his expression. It wouldn't be long now. However, he was already too far behind. She was going to climax first.

The path to her orgasm had found a fast lane of sorts. While Mary had always been good at pleasuring herself, she'd never gotten herself to the brink of orgasm this quickly before. It was like she had found a shortcut that had always been there but had never been used. By following it, Mary approached a special kind of ecstasy.

With Peter holding her head steady, Mary used both hands to pleasure herself and send herself over the edge. Instinct and desire took over. She didn't have to think about it. She didn't have to pursue it. The feeling just came to her.

When it arrived, a surge of heat shot up from her core, causing every muscle from her waist down to tense. Hot fluid coated her hand as her inner muscles contracted from the pleasure. Consequently, she sucked even harder in conjunction with each contraction. It ended up being just what Peter needed to achieve his peak.

"I'm coming, Mary. I'm coming. Keep...keep sucking. Swallow every last drop of my cum."

She barely heard him under the strength of her own orgasm, but Mary understood enough to give him what he wanted. His cock jerked within her mouth. Like a volcano preparing to erupt, it was ready to go off.

By the time it happened, her orgasm had mostly passed, allowing her to focus on finishing him. She removed a hand from between her thighs and grasped the base of Peter's cock again. She gave it a hard squeeze as she slowed down the rhythm, giving him a few more sucks. When she finally sent Peter over the threshold, he closed his eyes and threw his head back as he achieved his own ecstasy.

"Ohhh, Mary!" he cried out.

Still clutching her head, Peter let out a long, contented moan as he released his load. As requested, Mary kept his member securely in her mouth, ensuring that she would swallow every last drop.

The sheer volume of his cum actually surprised her. It must have been a while since he'd had a release. It once again tested her gag reflex, causing her to choke somewhat on the thick streams of warm, salty fluid.

Thankfully, her extensive experience allowed her to take it all without undermining the mood. If the look of euphoria on Peter's face was any indication, her efforts had paid off.

"Wow. Mary, that was... *Wow!*" Peter said breathlessly.

"I guess that means I kept my promise," Mary said after

finally releasing his cock from her mouth.

"Yeah...I'd say you did."

Mary smiled as he bathed in the feeling. She also made sure to be as through as possible, licking around the tip of his penis while stroking the base, extracting every last drop of cum.

In addition, Mary had taken a special satisfaction in what she'd done for him, as well. She didn't often accommodate a man like this, being so thorough with oral sex. For her, giving oral sex had been just a means to an end — something she'd done to get a man aroused or to entice him. She couldn't remember a time where she'd prioritized his pleasure over her own.

Remarkably enough, Mary had still gotten her share of pleasure out of it. It seemed so counterintuitive, but the results were undeniable.

Mary remained on her knees, smiling up at the contented man before her. He must have been just as surprised, because he actually laughed somewhat.

"You came, too, didn't you?" Peter said.

"You did tell me to touch myself while I blew you. I was just doing what you asked," Mary said innocently.

"Do you usually come that quickly?"

"No. I don't. I think that's a sign. Whatever we're doing here... It's working."

"I'll say. I think it's working well...in more ways than one," Peter said.

He had a cryptic undertone in his words, as if he'd sensed something in the moment that went beyond sex. Mary had experienced it, too. The emptiness that had plagued her for the past year had finally began to crack. Now, with Peter and the trust she had placed in him, Mary was ready to shatter it once and for all.

Chapter Sixteen

"Ready for the next step, Mary?" asked a seemingly content yet obviously unsatisfied Peter Rogers.

"I'm ready," Mary said.

There were no more doubts. What had started as a crazy idea had become a bold new path for Mary and Peter to confront their addiction. They had reversed their approach in exercising their sexual desires. Mary gave Peter full control over her, something she'd never dared give a man before and something no woman had ever given Peter. Whether it was crazy didn't matter at this point. Mary already knew beyond a shadow of a doubt that it was working.

By trusting him, she'd gotten more than basic pleasure in the form of a self-induced orgasm. New feelings had emerged, so much so that she'd struggled to keep up.

Even if it was successful so far, Mary needed more. Just giving Peter a blow job didn't make the experience complete. He clearly shared the sentiment. She sensed his mind racing again, going over all the options he had before him. Mary remained on her knees, trusting him to choose the right path for each of them.

"Help me get undressed," Peter said.

She eagerly complied. Still kneeling in front of him, Mary grabbed the sides of his pants, which were still around his knees, and pulled them down to his ankles. Peter offered some help, as well, kicking off his shoes along the way. That allowed her to completely remove them, socks and all.

"Now, stand up. Help me out of this shirt," Peter said.

Again, she complied. Her legs were still weak after her

orgasm but not weak enough to keep her from doing as he'd requested.

Now standing in the center of the living room, Peter rose to join her, kicking his pants to the side in the process. Sensing he couldn't get naked fast enough, Mary grabbed the hem of his shirt and pulled it over his head. It marked the first time outside her masturbation fantasies that she saw Peter Rogers in all his manly glory. Even though she had seen many naked men in her life, there was something about him that stuck her.

"Peter...wow," Mary said dazedly.

"Don't pretend to be impressed," Peter said.

"I'm not pretending."

He chuckled at her words, but Mary was dead serious. There was nothing half-hearted about her admiration of a naked Peter Rogers. Even with only the light from the gas fireplace and the occasional burst of lightning from outside, Mary saw a lot to admire.

This once-unremarkable boy had grown into a very handsome man. The pudge and flab that had once defined him had been replaced with a set of rock hard, six pack abs that looked like they had been taken from one of the old fitness magazines she'd modeled for. The ropy arms and weak shoulders had been replaced with bulging, well-defined muscles. Such a body made him more than equipped to carry out the duties of a firefighter.

However, she wanted his body to benefit him with more than just his chosen occupation. She'd placed her trust in him. She needed him to keep using it wisely.

"What do you want to do with me now, Peter?" Mary asked intently.

He didn't reply immediately. She couldn't tell if Peter was still mulling over his options or just enjoying the way she was looking at him.

He stepped closer to her so that his imposing form loomed over hers. There was no awkwardness this time. The tension that had plagued them before had been nullified—

yet another sign that they were doing something right.

"I'm going to kiss you now…and I want you to kiss back," he said with the utmost determination.

"I can do that," Mary said with a smile.

"I'm also going to touch you. I'm going to make you horny again. I'm going to make you want this sex even more than I do."

"That's not a challenge, is it?"

"No. It's a warning."

Confidence beamed from his every word. Inspired by it, he snaked one arm around her waist and cupped her chin with his hand. With laser-like focus, Peter captured her lips in a powerful kiss. Unlike before, there was no overwhelming shock or confusion. Mary knew what this was and where it would lead. She wanted it. He wanted it. There was nothing else to it. There didn't need to be.

They melded their lips and entwined their tongues. Mary embraced the feelings without hesitation. She slipped her arms around Peter's neck, allowing him to wrap her within his powerful embrace, naked flesh pressing against naked flesh. He roamed his hands over her body, tracing up her thighs and around her waist, paying special attention to her ass.

His intimate touch intensified the sensations while diverting her blood to all the right places. Mary had never let a man touch her so freely. She'd never let a man kiss her so firmly, either. She felt completely at his mercy, but it was not a mercy from which she wished to escape.

"Mary…" gasped Peter. He was so assertive, communicating his desire with every gesture. The way he said her name sent shivers down Mary's spine.

As she eagerly tasted his lips, the intense sensations mixed with the deepening pool of powerful feelings. The emotions blurred the line between lust, love, affection, desire and everything in between. Like unlocking doors that had never been opened, the feelings overwhelmed her in all the right ways.

As she and Peter made out in the middle of the living room, Mary's legs became weak. A powerful heat formed in her core. Whatever desire she'd released with her previous orgasm was replaced with entirely new sensations. She could tell by the way Peter's cock began to stiffen again that he shared in that sentiment. When he abruptly broke the kiss, she knew they had reached a point of no return.

"Tell me you want this, Mary," Peter said, his hands firmly on her ass.

"I want this, Peter," Mary said, as though it were a reflex.

"Tell me. Tell me *how much* you want it."

"I want it, Peter…so much."

"Tell me more," he urged.

"I want you to fuck me. I want to have sex with you… make love to you…*everything!*" The words came out of her mouth with little input from her brain. Wherever they came from, they got the point across. Still cupping her chin, Peter smiled with burning intent.

"That's exactly what I'm going to do," he said to her. "I'm going take you in my arms, carry you into my bedroom and give you what you want. But I'm going to do it *my* way."

"I understand," Mary said.

"Then you don't need to say another word. I'll take it from here."

She nodded to acknowledge his command, effectively sealing the deal. With the utmost confidence, Peter kissed her again to silence any possible reservations—not that Mary had any left at this point. He lifted her off the floor. Mary instinctively hitched her legs around his waist. All she could do was hold on and let Peter take her to their fate.

The fervor of their kissing intensified as they stormed into his bedroom. As soon as they entered, he kicked the door shut and carried her over to the queen-sized bed. He even pulled back the covers and sheets before he laid her down, right in the middle.

Peter gained even more leverage in the process, hovering over her with his imposing body as she lay on the bed.

He continued making good use of his position, tracing his hands up her waist and giving more attention to her breasts. As he kissed her, he squeezed and kneaded her fleshy mounds in a way that made Mary gasp.

Looming over her in the dim light of the room, he looked so powerful. However, Mary didn't feel nervous. The feelings he conveyed turned any potential anxiety into a deeper arousal.

The heat in her core continued to spread and Peter's cock was growing as well, but she also sensed a growing impatience in him. He didn't want to just fuck her. He really wanted to do it *his* way. Breaking the kiss and breathing heavily with desire, he looked down at Mary with a penetrating gaze.

"I'm going to eat your pussy now," Peter said.

Mary didn't even nod this time and he didn't wait for her response, either. He immediately resumed the kissing, starting at her neck and trailing his way down her body.

She didn't dare move an inch. The feeling of his lips on other parts of her flesh sent more shivers down her spine. Mary gasped with anticipation, feeling him pass over her breasts, down her torso and over her navel. If this were a typical sexual encounter, Mary would've started barking orders by now, telling him where and how to pleasure her. She stayed silent this time, trusting that Peter knew what he was doing.

It didn't make the wait any less agonizing. At one point, he stopped just a few inches from her folds. Mary instinctively parted her legs to allow him to position his head between her thighs.

"Peter...please!" Mary said desperately.

Hearing her plea seemingly emboldened him even more. He could have made her beg even harder, could have tormented her with the promise of more pleasure. In the end, Peter didn't undermine the trust she'd placed in him.

He grabbed hold of her thighs to push her legs even farther apart. Then he buried his face in her pussy.

Her body tensed as he made contact with her outer folds. "Ooh, Peter!" gasped Mary.

"Mmm...so good," Peter said after he'd tasted her.

His experience in orally pleasuring women showed. Peter knew the intricacies of female anatomy. However, Mary doubted any of those women had felt anything like this.

His teasing of her clit sent Mary's body into a frenzy. Hot sensations shot through her body, spreading sensual shocks like waves crashing against the shoreline. She savored every one of them as though they were a long-overdue treat. She even supplemented them in her own way, fondling her breasts and elevating her hips so Peter could maximize his efforts.

Those efforts paid off. The feelings intensified, the waves on that proverbial shore growing larger by the second. It ignited a potent mix of pleasure and passion in Mary.

"You're getting so wet. You want it, don't you?" Peter said, briefly looking up from her dripping cunt.

"Mmm..." was all Mary could get out.

Peter laughed at her response and went back to probing deeper with his tongue and stirring that growing fire within her. He alternated nipping her clit and her pussy with an energy that would not be tamed.

Once he'd brought her to the brink of another orgasm several times and had left her just at the edge, Peter lifted his head. The bottom of his face was shiny with her juices when he gave her a self-satisfied grin and lowered her ass to the bed. Then he crawled back over her and gazed at her with intense desire. She could feel a fresh and very hard erection pressing against her.

"So hard already?" Mary asked, still dazed with the need to come.

"Don't look so shocked. Nobody ever became a sex addict by being easily satisfied," Peter said.

It was still pretty impressive. Most men couldn't get hard so quickly after coming. Then again, Peter wasn't most men.

"Or maybe we should both be shocked. Doing things like

this—doing them so differently... It makes me feel so many things. It's bound to have certain effects," Peter said, now caressing her face.

"That's for sure," Mary replied, hungry for even greater ecstasy.

Still breathing heavily, Peter aligned his rock-hard penis with the entrance to her vagina, heightening the anticipation. He appeared poised to seize what he wanted, and Mary was oh-so-willing.

"I'm going to enter you now," he told her.

"I'm ready, Peter," Mary said.

His gaze remained locked with hers, conveying the breadth of his desires. Mary grabbed on to his shoulders and let Peter do the honors.

With a single thrust, his hard cock penetrated her cunt. She immediately let out a sharp gasp as her inner muscles stretched to accommodate his dick. His entry was remarkably smooth, a testament to just how wet and ready she was. As he buried himself deeper into her core, a rush of sensations shot through Mary's body.

"Peter...that feels so good," Mary gasped.

"Oh, Mary...so hot and tight." Peter moaned.

They had officially reached the end of the path. Peter had done just as he'd said he would do. He'd told Mary he was going to take her into his bed and have sex with her his way—a way that had aligned his needs with hers. However, the act was anything but complete.

"I'm going to fuck you now," Peter said.

"Oh, yes...please!" Mary urged.

For a brief moment, Mary just savored the feeling of Peter's hard cock filling her. She might be a recovering sex addict, but she hadn't forgotten how good it felt. Peter clearly hadn't forgotten, either. He began moving his hips in a steady pistoning motion.

It was so familiar to her, having sex with a handsome stud of a man, but this time with Peter gave Mary a feeling that was so much more than basic pleasure. She'd shared herself, not just her body. She'd opened up old wounds, let him into her world—literally and figuratively—at a time when she'd felt so vulnerable. The feeling, sharing a connection that was both passionate and physical, evoked more than just pleasure.

As the intensity grew, the moment really sank in for Mary. She was having sex with Peter Rogers. After a year of battling her addiction, she had officially relapsed. However, this didn't seem like simply that. She knew all too well what meaningless sex felt like. This was anything but meaningless.

"We... We're doing it, Peter. We're really doing it!" cried Mary.

She doubted he'd heard her. He was directing all his passionate energy toward her, manifesting in every sensual motion. It made Mary the center of his universe, the one person with whom he dared to be so intimate...so close. The desire for greater pleasure mixed with the need to embrace this man completely—body, heart and soul. It intensified the powerful experience, guiding her into a world of bliss into which even a hardened sex addict had never ventured.

"Peter...I feel you...so deep," she said through her moans. She'd never experienced this before...ever. What she felt went beyond the physical element. This wasn't just lust, wasn't just pleasure. Overwhelming emotions and unexpected feelings took on a new dimension.

Mary shifted her hands from his shoulders to his face. As she caressed him tenderly, he smiled back. Then, while he was still fucking her, he captured her lips in another kiss.

These were not simple acts of lust and desire. While those feelings were present, Mary was experiencing something more. *Could it just be love? Could it be that basic?* The connection she felt with Peter went well beyond the feelings that had fueled her addiction.

"Oh, Mary...you're so beautiful," Peter said.

It was the simplest compliment a man could give a woman, but it worked for her.

The kissing, the pumping and the moaning became more chaotic. Mary barely noticed the thunder and lightning flashing outside, which occasionally filled the room with blinding light, illuminating the moment.

As it played out, Mary drifted closer and closer to that special peak…the very height of pleasure that she'd known so well but never quite this way. Peter carried her into a special place, one reserved for a feeling this exquisite. As it approached, her heart and her passions became one and the same.

"Peter, I…I'm getting close again. I…I'm getting *real* close!" Mary said.

"Good," Peter said. "I want you to come. In fact, I'm going to *make* you come again!" He said those words with such certainty that it wasn't a promise as much as it was a declaration.

Peter had once again exercised his control over their act. He briefly withdrew from her, transferred his grip to her waist then turned her over so that she was on her hands and knees with her ass pointed right at him. She grabbed on to the headboard of the bed for support, holding on as Peter positioned himself behind her and aligned himself with her pussy. Without hesitation, he thrust back into her and resumed the same rhythm as before. This time, he pounded her with greater urgency.

"Ooh, so…so hard! So…so strong!" cried Mary.

Hearing her moans must have strengthened his resolve. Peter's grunts seemed more determined. The sound of his pelvis smacking against her ass filled the room, drowning out the sound of the rain and thunder echoing from the raging storm outside.

He reached between her legs with one hand and massaged her swollen clitoris. With every thrust, Peter stimulated Mary in just the right way to send her on an accelerated path to ecstasy.

"Ohhh, I…I'm coming, Peter!" Mary exclaimed. "I'm coming again! I—"

Her desperate cries devolved into a single, powerful moan of euphoria. She clutched the headboard, arched and threw her head back as more powerful heat erupted within her core. It spread in every direction as her inner muscles convulsed around Peter's cock. He steadied his hips and tightened his hold on her as orgasmic bliss surged through her body.

"That's it, Mary. Come for me," urged Peter.

Mary barely heard his words, but she felt his sentiment. Just as before, the sensations conveyed something beyond physical pleasure.

Waves of ecstasy coursed through Mary as Peter wrapped his arms around her, holding her close during her venture into ecstasy. He lifted her into an upright position, allowing her to let go of the headboard. Then he kissed around her neck, evoking more contented purrs as her climax subsided.

"Did you enjoy that?" he asked as he nibbled around her ear.

"Yes…I did," replied Mary in a post-orgasmic haze.

"You're so easy to please. I'm…not used to that. The women I've slept were never this…eager," Peter said. "I guess that makes you special."

"Or…it makes *us* special."

"Good point. Makes me wonder…just how special."

His words had some powerful connotations. He must have felt what she had, the deeper emotions emerging from their intimate act. The depths of those feelings had finally reached the void that had once plagued her. It must have been just as profound for him.

"I've done what I set out to do. Now, you're going to return the favor," Peter said, once again speaking in a definitive tone.

"It's only fair," Mary said. "How do you want me?"

"First, I'm going to lie down on my back. I want you to get on top of me, ride my dick and ride it *hard*. And I want you to keep doing it until I come. Do you understand?"

"Yes. I understand perfectly." Mary grinned.

She was still short of breath and her sex was still sensitive from her climaxes. That wouldn't prevent her from giving him the pleasure he wanted. He'd made good on all the trust she had placed in him. She intended to return the favor.

Having articulated his desires clearly, Peter released Mary from his grip and withdrew his still-hard cock. He then reversed their positions so that he was lying on his back while Mary hovered over him. This put her in the optimum position to regain some leverage.

She'd always jumped at the opportunity to seize such advantage over a man in the pursuit of more pleasure. This time, however, that crossed her mind only for the briefest moment. Instead, her ecstasy became secondary.

Despite some lingering weakness in her legs, she prepared herself for more fucking. When she was aligned perfectly, she reached behind her and grasped his member so she could guide it into her pussy.

"Mmm...you're inside me again, Peter," Mary said as his member filled her depths.

"Still so hot," Peter said with a content moan. "Go on. Start riding me."

Heeding his desires, Mary began moving her hips. She put her hands firmly on Peter's waist. She leaned forward slightly, dug her feet into the bed and began riding his dick as he'd commanded.

As soon as Mary established a rhythm, she stepped up the pace. She moved her hips fervently, her wet folds gliding up and down the rigid length of his cock. His expression shifted as he slipped into a blissful daze, not unlike the one she'd seen earlier when she'd given him oral sex. Seeing him enjoy it made Mary smile.

It didn't bother her that she was pushing herself to the point of strain. She didn't even try for another orgasm herself. Giving Peter the pleasure he wanted meant pushing her desires into uncharted territory. Mary entered that domain without a shred of doubt.

"Yeah, that's it! *That's* what I want—what I need," Peter said through blissful moans.

His reaction prompted Mary to ride him harder, pushing her physical and sexual stamina to new heights. She let her body do most of the work while her mind shut out her limitations.

As she rode his member with great vigor, Peter reached for her hips and grasped them firmly, guiding her movements and adding more intensity to the rhythm. He supplemented her efforts as well, bucking his hips upward to drive his cock deeper into her depths.

She conveyed every bit of sexual energy into Peter that she could muster, breasts bouncing and hips gyrating with every motion. At one point, Peter transferred his hands from her hips to her breasts and kneaded them firmly, pinching her nipples and sending shots of pleasure through her. Even though he had prioritized his pleasure over hers, he was still willingly sharing it.

That made Mary push herself even harder. Her pelvis smacked against his, echoing over the jumbled noise of his moans and the ongoing storm outside. Such intensity turned his blissful moans into determined grunts.

"Mary…so good. It feels so good," Peter said in a haze of pleasure. "I'm almost there."

She kept riding him, working her hips and rocking the bed. His cock was so hard, clearly aching for a release. She also saw the expression on Peter's face shift and contort with the sensations. He never once closed his eyes, remaining completely focused on her. In those eyes, Mary saw something striking.

He *needed* this. Something about being the woman he seized it with filled Mary with a satisfaction that went beyond physical pleasure.

Mary had already experienced these sensations when she'd come. Peter deserved to feel them, too. She couldn't begin to make sense of them. She didn't bother trying. Her only focus at this point was giving him the climax he needed and all the emotions that would come with it.

Driven by this purpose, Mary released her grip on Peter's waist and placed her hands atop his, still on her breasts. As she continued to ride him, she leaned back a little and really let her hips grind against his. That gave Peter the final push he needed.

"Ohhh, I'm coming, Mary!" exclaimed Peter. "Slow down. Hold it…right there. I'm going to — "

That was all he could get out. He had already crossed the threshold where the light trickles of pleasure became a raging torrent. Mary didn't need him to give any orders at that point. She could sense what he needed and she let his ecstasy guide her.

His restraint obviously shattered when Peter arched, transferring his hands back to her hips. He closed his eyes and let out a deep, prolonged moan. Mary accommodated him every step of the way, ceasing her fervent motions and steadying her hips.

His cock throbbed and pulsed inside her as streams of hot cum shot into her depths. While she didn't experience an orgasm, watching Peter achieve that feeling gave her a whole new perspective. In that moment, his pleasure and her pleasure became one and the same.

"I feel it, too, Peter," Mary said breathlessly. "But it's more…"

She wasn't sure if he'd heard her or understood what she'd meant. It didn't matter at this point. Mary just smiled and watched Peter.

She caressed his face and held him so he could revel in the sensations.

"Mary…" Peter said, still in a blissful daze.

"Shh… I want you to enjoy this," Mary said.

He smiled back and even laughed. It proved to Mary that he was experiencing what she'd felt. It hadn't been just an overdue orgasm. There had been an intimacy to this, one that'd been missing from both of their lives. He'd felt it. This powerful outburst of desire wouldn't have been so profound if he hadn't.

He loosened his grip on her. She instinctively rose off him, remaining within his arms as their tired bodies gave out. Together, they fell back on the bed where Mary eagerly curled up next to him. His flesh radiated an amazing warmth in his post-orgasmic glow, one in which she eagerly immersed herself.

"Wow. That was..." Peter said, his words quickly trailing off.

"I know," Mary said.

"I mean it. I'm not just saying it. That really was..."

"I know, Peter. I *know*."

He laughed again. Mary found herself laughing with him. Being in this bed together like this, their bodies entwined after such a profound feeling, defied everything she'd thought she'd known about sex and intimacy. As they lingered in their powerful embrace, a series of bright lightning strikes illuminated the whole room. In that flash, the breadth of the experience sank in.

"Can you at least *try* to put it into words? Because...I'm a loss here," he said.

"I'd love to, but I'm going to need a moment. I'm still a bit...winded," Mary said.

"Should I apologize?"

"You'd better not," she said. "What we just did...how we did it...why we did it... It *worked*."

"It worked?" Peter said, still somewhat confused.

"Yes. It did. I feel it. I don't know how I know it, but I do."

Mary said the words without much thought. At some point, she would have to scrutinize them, but not now. It wouldn't change anything. She was entirely convinced. What she and Peter had done had *worked*—in more ways than they ever could've imagined.

"I definitely felt something—something I've never experienced before," Peter said in a more serious tone.

"The feeling is mutual. You know how to set yourself apart, Peter," Mary said.

"I still want to understand it. I want to know that what we just did wasn't a fluke."

"It wasn't."

"But I—"

Mary placed a finger over his lips to silence him. Peter was overthinking the situation way too much for a man who'd just had sex. She couldn't process everything about these feelings for him, but she could certainly prove that it hadn't been a fluke.

"Maybe this will convince you," Mary said.

In an act that coincided with another flash of lightning, Mary gave Peter powerful kiss that she hoped conveyed the necessary feelings to quell any lingering doubts he might have.

That should stop him from overthinking the situation. This is real. God help us, this is real.

What they'd just experienced was pure and genuine. For Mary, all those years she'd spent in the brutal cycles of addiction had finally culminated in that moment. Now, the cycle had been broken. For the first time in her life, she felt truly complete.

When she broke the kiss, Mary knew by the look on his face that it had done its job.

"Yes, Mary," he said with the widest grin she had seen to date, "it definitely worked."

Chapter Seventeen

When can an addict say they've been cured? Is it even possible? Is the very concept of addiction flawed to begin with?

These questions had been burning in Mary's mind, but she didn't have the energy to answer them. In fact, she didn't have the energy to do much of anything after she and Peter had shared such an amazing experience.

It had become something of a blur after that final kiss. Mary hadn't remembered saying much else after that. They'd slipped into a blissful daze, drunk on the new feelings, fallen back onto the bed, crawled under the sheets and shared more affectionate gestures.

They'd kissed, fondled and explored each other's bodies. It had alternated between simple touching and full-blown foreplay. It had even led to a few additional sex acts. Mary had surprised herself, and Peter for that matter, but a lack of sex over the past year had created a lot of pent-up desire. Being the wonderful man he was, Peter was happy to help her release it. All the feelings and pleasures they had shared only heightened the overall experience. It eventually had gotten to a point where she'd made another stunning realization.

"Damn it, Peter. I think I'm in *love* with you," she'd said.

Mary remembered seeing a beaming grin on his face when she'd said that. Then, he'd kissed her again and led to even more passionate expressions.

Throughout the sex acts that had followed, one sentiment had become clear. Her fate was now inevitably tied to that of Peter Rogers.

Eventually, they'd worn themselves out and had fallen

into a light slumber. Mary remembered curling up next to him and feeling more content than she had at any point in her adult life. She would've been perfectly content remaining in this state. "Thank you, Peter Rogers. Thank you for making me feel so…complete," were the last words she said before she fell asleep in his arms.

* * * *

She woke to the cold feeling of not being in Peter's embrace anymore. Drowsy and still a bit sore, she rose to see Peter sitting on the edge of the bed, leaning back on his arms and staring out of his bedroom window. It was still raining outside, but not nearly as hard as before. He looked lost in thought but still very much content.

"Hey," Peter said in a casual tone.

"Hey," replied Mary, holding the sheets to her naked body. "Couldn't sleep?"

"It's still daylight out," he teased. "You didn't wear me out that much."

"Guess I'll have to try harder next time."

"I know you will. You're still a competitor."

"That I am," Mary said proudly.

This might be the most comfortable she had ever felt with someone after sex. She was downright giddy, like a kid who'd finally gotten to go outside again after being sick. With renewed energy, Mary crawled from under the sheets and embraced Peter from behind. He accepted the gesture and eagerly returned it by grasping her hands with his.

They were still naked. Having become so familiar with each other's bodies, Mary felt no inclination to change that. She rested her chin on his shoulder and gazed out of the window with him. There was an eerie beauty to watching the rain fall. Even the thunder and lightning were strangely soothing and not just because it was ending a drought.

"You know, at some point, you'll have to give me back my clothes. You don't want me walking home naked in this weather," Mary said.

"I'll throw them in the dryer once the power comes back on," Peter said.

"And if the power *doesn't* come back on?"

"Then I guess you'll just have to stay here at my place and remain naked for the rest of the night."

"If that's how it has to be, I'll make do," Mary said with a fake sigh.

"If it makes you feel better, I'll stay naked," Peter said.

"You don't have to, but I know you're too nice a guy to avoid sharing the burden."

"It's no burden at all. I wouldn't avoid it if it was. You're worth it, Mary...for all the right reasons."

She had heard that kind of sweet-talk from men before, but she'd never believed it beyond a certain point. When Peter said it, Mary believed it implicitly. She even gave him a kiss on the cheek to show her appreciation.

He gave her hand a light squeeze to acknowledge her gesture, but he remained deep in thought. Mary could sense his mind racing. He didn't seem conflicted, but something was clearly brewing.

"I normally don't ask guys what they're thinking after sex. They tend to find it annoying. This time, though, I'm genuinely curious," Mary said.

"A lot of women I've slept with pretend to be curious, but I know you're not," Peter said.

"I'm not a fan of faking interest...or other things," she said coyly.

"I wasn't going to keep it to myself, anyway. I think this is something we need to talk about at some point. It might as well be now."

"Naked, in bed and during a blackout? That's as good a time we're going to get," Mary said.

Peter remained deadly serious. He might not have been conflicted, but this was clearly important to him. That made it important to Mary, too. Afterglow aside, they were in this together.

"I have a theory," Peter said.

"About what?" Mary asked.

"About our addiction and why what we just did worked so damn well," he replied.

"Then by all means...share it. I'll even help you test it."

"Not sure that's necessary. I've been testing it in my head since I woke up. It's not perfect, but it makes too much sense."

He sparked Mary's intrigue.

"Stop me if I say something stupid, but I need to talk this out. From what I've gathered, most people become addicted to something when it fills a need of sorts," began Peter. "It doesn't have to make sense. You don't even have to know what that need is. It just needs to fill it."

"That's not stupid. Even hardcore addicts would agree with that," Mary said.

"For some people, it's drugs. For others, it's gambling. For us, it was sex."

"Was?" questioned Mary.

"Sorry. I'm getting ahead of myself here, but bear with me, because this is where it gets tricky...and *awkward*."

"We're both naked. Awkward is a relative concept at this point."

"Point taken, but I'm not talking about the kind of awkwardness that comes with being naked. I'm talking about the kind we don't notice until it's shoved in our face," Peter said. "We both followed a similar path to addiction. We were in environments that gave us too many opportunities to pursue it. We were in a state that made us too vulnerable to avoid it. We let it get *so* bad that it took something extreme to give us that moment of clarity that every addict dreads."

"I want to say that's a hell of a coincidence, but it's the basic story behind every addiction," Mary said. "I've lost count of how many times I've heard it over the past year."

"Then it's the finer details that we need to focus on. It's those fine details that made what we just did work so damn well."

His tone shifted, not sounding quite as serious anymore. It was strange, but in a good way. Whenever Peter overanalyzed something, he often got too serious. Mary used to find that annoying, but now it might be the key to understanding this.

"Looking at it now, we know it wasn't just the sex that we were addicted to. It was the way we did it," continued Peter. "That brutal cycle we described... It was actually worse than we thought."

"That cycle made us miserable and got people killed. How could it possibly be worse?" wondered Mary.

"It's easy when you don't see the forest for the trees. You described—in graphic detail, mind you—how you fueled this cycle."

"You weren't exactly subtle, either, Mr. I'm-A-Sexy-Firefighter," Mary said.

"Very true, but beside the point," he retorted. "When we did what we did, we thought we were doing it the way we should. I thought it was the best thing for a man to just let the woman be in charge during sex. That's the only way I thought I could accomplish my goals."

"And I accomplished mine by doing the same, but from the opposite end of the spectrum," Mary said. "I still don't know why I did it like that, but that's how I did. I think we just proved that our logic was flawed."

"That's where my theory comes in. You see, I think inverting our approach to sex revealed something else. By doing something so radically different, we found out that what we had been doing before was...incomplete."

That idea that she'd briefly considered earlier struck Mary anew. Just a few weeks ago, she'd lamented over the festering emptiness she had felt for the past year. That void had made the scars of her addiction feel every bit as bad as the addiction itself. Sister Angela and the program could only do so much to treat it.

Then Peter Rogers had come along, and for the first time

in years, she hadn't felt so incomplete. After struggling to cope with her problems, it was refreshing. She didn't necessarily need an explanation, but it still couldn't hurt to understand it.

"It all comes back to how we pursue our goals," Peter said. "You and I are both big on goals — some might say to an unhealthy level."

"Not going to argue *that*," Mary said. "Not sure it makes for a functional theory, though."

"It's not the only variable, but it's an important one to consider. When we're young and horny, sex is a goal in and of itself. There's really not much to it. That's why it wasn't that big a problem when we were teenagers."

"My high school guidance counselor might beg to differ, but she also claimed I had no future in being a model, so to hell with her," Mary said.

"The problem only came when we got older," Peter said. "Our goals changed. They became more mature, as well, so to speak. That extended to sex."

"You think we underestimated the maturity of a couple of horny twenty-somethings?" Mary asked.

"Actually, I think the opposite happened. I think we overestimated it."

That surprised Mary. She gave him a curious look, but he remained serious. He'd never claimed his theory was simple or intuitive. Still intrigued, Mary gave him a chance to prove it.

"We *thought* we knew what we wanted and how to get it. We even got really good at it, as our many sexual conquests can attest," Peter said.

"Some can attest more than others, I imagine," added Mary.

"Very true," he continued, "but the problem wasn't the conquests themselves. The problem was that what we *thought* we wanted wasn't consistent with what we *actually* wanted."

"So, we didn't really want what we thought we wanted?

I'm a little confused," Mary said.

"That's a sign, in and of itself. You see, as we matured, I think we wanted more than mutual orgasms. I think we wanted the same thing that most people — as in most *non-addicted* people — want from sex."

"Which is..." Mary said.

"Intimacy," he answered.

On the surface, it sounded cheesy. It gave the impression that she and Peter had been callous with sex. Mary didn't accept that at first. If anyone else had said that, she would've been insulted. The more she considered it, though, the more it made sense.

She thought back to some of the many men she'd been with over the years. While there were plenty of casual hook-ups, Mary recalled a few occasions where she'd let herself get passionate. Before today, she would've called that intimate. Now, in wake of what she and Peter had just shared, she could call those past experiences a lot of things, but she couldn't call them intimate.

"This is where this crazy theory becomes harsh reality," Peter said in a more distant tone.

"It's hardly crazy. It's already making more sense than I expected," Mary said.

"That still doesn't make the reality any less harsh. That need for intimacy really clashed with our desire to avoid any entanglements. I don't know where that desire came from. For me, it might have just been me trying to be better than all the other guys who hooked up with beautiful women. For you? Well, I don't want to speculate, but that stuff with your family might have played a part."

"No need to get Freudian on me, Peter. I know what you mean. Does the reason really matter, though?"

"In the long run? Not really," answered Peter. "Whatever our reason, we didn't change our approach to match our desires. We wanted intimacy, but we kept pursuing the same shallow romps, ensuring we never actually got what we wanted."

"I'm seeing the signs of that brutal cycle again," Mary said. "We find someone, we have sex with them and we don't get everything we want. Then we find someone else and do it again in the exact same way. We *still* don't get it. Then, we try it again…and again…and again."

"I noticed those signs, too. I guess that means we're on the same page now. That means I can skip to the most critical part of my theory."

The tone of Peter's voice had changed, taking on a more emotional subtext. He shifted where he sat, turning around so that he faced her. Mary shifted as well so she sat with him near the center of the bed, atop the ruffled sheets.

In the dim lighting provided by the window, he gazed at her in a way that got her heart racing again. Mary did her best to calm herself, but only succeeded in part as Peter took her hands in his once more, conveying the very *intimacy* they'd failed to achieve before.

In him, Mary saw a man in the midst of an emotional epiphany. There was no more speculation. He had the glint of a man full of utter certainty.

"On this day — this crazy day when a record storm rolled through — we tried a different approach. We tried something other than the way that made us a couple of miserable, broken sex addicts," Peter said with a hint of excitement in his tone.

"And it worked," Mary said with a smile.

"You're right. It did, but not just because it was so different. I believe — in fact, I'm *convinced* — that it worked because we did something we'd avoided doing for most of our adult lives. We placed our faith in one another."

"Faith? I thought we just trusted each other to try a crazy idea."

"Trust is basic. We can trust the chef at a restaurant not to spit in our food. We can even trust people to not do anything crazy during sex. To have faith in someone? Well, that requires more than trust. It also happens to be the key ingredient for intimacy."

He released his grip on Mary's hands and caressed her face. His excitement had turned to affection. Her heart rate jumped, this time in a way she could not temper. She had heard people talk about faith before. Sister Angela preached about it endlessly, so much so that she had tuned it out for the most part. The faith Peter described felt far more personal and far more profound than any theology.

The power of that faith became clearer in his warm touch. She couldn't grasp or quantify it, but it felt so real. Those feelings that had emerged with Peter during sex took on a whole new dimension.

"I placed my faith in you, Mary," Peter said strongly. "Even before we had sex, I shared my burdens with you. I had every inclination to keep pushing everybody away, but you changed that. I made myself vulnerable with you. Then, you gave me a chance to make myself strong."

"Which required a lot of faith on my part," Mary said.

"Which is exactly what turns trust into intimacy," he said with growing conviction. "By giving me control of our sex, you had to do more than trust. You had to believe that I would give you wanted...be it genuine intimacy or multiple orgasms."

"And you succeeded...on both counts," Mary said proudly.

"Beyond the success, we finally achieved something we had been missing—something we'd tried to seize in all the wrong ways for all the wrong reasons. The burden that drove my addiction? I see it now for what it really is. Because of you, Mary Ann Scott, I *know* what I want, what I need and why I need it. But most importantly, I know *who* I want to share it with."

His touch became more affectionate. There was no stopping the emotions at this point, so Mary didn't bother trying. Another lump formed in her throat as tears welled up in her eyes. It overwhelmed her, the way this man talked to her and the way he conveyed so many feelings. She finally began to understand the breadth of those emotions.

As she struggled to steady the flow, Mary slipped onto his lap and wrapped her arms around his neck. Peter smiled warmly at her intimate embrace. A few quick flashes of lightning illuminated the extent of that intimacy, as if nature itself wanted to emphasize the feeling. Mary heard that message loud and clear. It inspired her to take yet another leap of faith.

"Peter, I think you've done more than enough to prove your theory," declared Mary. "You can stop trying to convince me. I believe you."

"So…is this your way of saying you're convinced," Peter said, still smiling.

"Actually, I like to think I'm adding to your theory. All this talk of intimacy and faith… It reminds me of something I blurted out while drunk on great sex. I don't know if you heard it, but…I said at one point I was falling in love with you."

Saying it out loud in a coherent state of mind made her heart skip a beat. A year ago, just hinting at it was enough to make her pull away from someone. That couldn't happen this time. Neither she nor Peter dared avoid this. The way he looked at her and the way he kept embracing her evoked even more emotions. She would've liked a moment or two to catch up with her thoughts and feelings, but Mary was beyond caring at this point.

"I did hear it," Peter said.

"I think that's something else we didn't know we wanted. Between faith and intimacy, it's just one of those byproducts I don't think we can avoid," Mary said.

"I don't want to avoid it."

"Me, neither…because it reveals something else that I don't think I can avoid," she said. "The day you showed up at the program, I was a hollow shell of a woman. I berated myself for feeling so empty and miserable."

"Why would you do that to yourself?" Peter asked.

"Because I didn't understand the emptiness I felt. Hell, I didn't even try to understand it. Then, you came along. I connected with you. I trusted. No, I placed my *faith* in you. In that moment, I felt the emptiness begin to fade. Those feelings I had been missing? The ones I kept searching for, but never found? I began to feel them."

At this point, Mary was ready to break down and cry. Peter supported her, keeping her strong with his embrace and his affection. She fought off more tears but never stopped smiling. She ended up leaning her forehead against Peter's, reaching for his hands and letting their fingers become entwined. Another round of lightning outside revealed the passion in his eyes.

"So...do you really want to share this with me? This faith and intimacy that we've finally found?" Mary asked, her voice still strained.

"Without a doubt...I do," answered Peter, not hesitating in the slightest.

"That's all well and good. We'll fill that void. We'll end the brutal cycle that fueled our addiction. The only major side-effect is...I'll be madly in love with you. You think you can handle that?"

"Seeing as how I started falling in love with you the moment I confirmed my theory? Hell, yeah, I can handle it."

Through all the emotions and tears, Mary laughed with him as the final shred of emptiness faded. The powerful experience was truly complete, but its effects were just beginning. In a moment that sealed a new fate for her and Peter, she leaned in and kissed him again.

She was falling in love with him. He was falling in love with her. She, Mary Ann Scott—a recovering sex addict— was falling in love with Peter Rogers, another recovering sex addict. No theory could make it less crazy, but Mary didn't care. She was beyond caring. This was good. *This* was right.

Even if she were falling in love with Peter, though, it didn't change the truth. She had relapsed. She and Peter were entering unknown territory. Could a couple of recovering sex addicts be in love? Could that love even work? Mary didn't have the strength to process all these feelings and — if his grip on her was any indication—neither did Peter. At the very least, she had faith that they would figure it out together.

Epilogue

Not long ago, Hartman County had been in the midst of a record drought and Mary Ann Scott had been plagued by a crippling emptiness. Then, a powerful storm had come and ended that drought. Fittingly enough, an equally powerful force had come along in Peter Robert Rogers. What could've been a relapse had turned into something so much more.

He had finally shattered the cycle that had fueled her addiction. In him, she hadn't just found someone who could end the cycle. She'd found someone who could warm her heart, her bed and everything in between.

She was in love with him. Moreover, she was expressing that love in a way that felt both right and blissful. In one fateful moment, sex had turned from an addiction into a catalyst — a familiar feeling that had inspired new passions. Those passions had filled the hole in her soul that had been plaguing her for nearly a year. It was almost fitting that it had taken a full-blown relapse to realize them.

"You want more eggs, Mary?" Peter asked, carrying himself as though he'd just put out a hundred forest fires.

"That depends. Are you going to smother them in tabasco sauce?" quipped Mary coyly.

"I put tabasco sauce on your ice cream once when we were kids. I think I know now how to smother you properly."

"You've seen me naked, so I guess you've earned a little trust," she teased.

"Just a little?"

"You'd rather I stop challenging you?"

"Hell, no!" Peter answered without hesitation.

Mary shared a good laugh with her lover as he served her

a second helping of scrambled eggs. She'd needed a hardy meal this morning. The previous night had proven to be a real workout—and not just physically. It marked the latest in a string of exhausting nights with him, but Mary wasn't complaining.

Sitting at Peter's kitchen table, wearing only her panties and one of his T-shirts, she couldn't be more satisfied...in more ways than one. Since that fateful day they'd come together, two broken souls struggling with addiction, they had gone through an adjustment period of sorts. It had been a hell of one in that they'd made it a point to do things differently, even after they'd had sex. What she and Peter shared went beyond sex. That meant approaching everything from a new perspective.

With sex addicts, it was never just about having great sex. If anything, it was often a secondary concern at most. In Mary's experience, sex just kept the cycle going. One physically satisfying night set up the next. Such a wonderful night only motivated her to seek another. It was a never-ending, inherently destructive path without emotional fulfillment that had nearly destroyed her soul.

Peter had walked that path too. He didn't hide his own emotional scars. For him, they were still raw. For her, they had been festering for nearly a year. Great sex only did so much to heal those scars. The greater passions beyond it did so much more.

Those passions drove them to start a new direction, one they could forge together. That meant spending more nights together. After that first time, they'd actually sat down together the next morning—in their underwear, no less—and put together a crude but ambitious plan. For the next two weeks, they'd spend the nights together.

Those nights couldn't just be spent having sex, though. They had to actually open up to each other, taking turns being vulnerable. That meant talking about uncomfortable moments in their past while being brutally honest about how they felt, what they wanted out of this new relationship and how they were going to go about it.

It reminded Mary of a workout regimen, setting up goals and laying out schedules. It might not have been the most romantic approach, but it put them in a position to confront their vulnerabilities. As with her workout routines, Mary had stuck to it and so had Peter. The results already spoke for themselves.

With a fresh plate of eggs—properly smothered in tabasco sauce—now sitting in front of her, Peter joined her at the table. He also had a helping of eggs and hash-browns, the same protein-rich meal she'd laid out for him when they had been kids. Studying him wearing only a pair of sweatpants, leaving his upper body exposed in the morning sun, Mary decided it was a hell of a way to start the day.

"I gotta say, Peter, I could get used to this," Mary said after taking a bite. "All this—waking up with you in the morning, having breakfast and wearing your clothes—it's really starting to grow on me."

"Good thing. My clothes look better on you, anyway," he teased.

"I'm serious."

"So am I…and I'm not just talking about my clothes," he said in a more somber tone. "This feels so right. Corny, but right."

"I know. That's what kind of scares me."

"Scares you?" Peter asked curiously.

Mary put her fork down and set her eggs aside, which said a lot in and of itself because she was still pretty hungry. This was more important, though. With a serious but loving gaze, she reached over and placed her hand on Peter's arm.

"It's not that kind of scared, I promise you," Mary assured him. "You haven't been a recovering addict for as long as I have. That means you don't have to spend an entire year with a gaping hole in your soul, not knowing how you're ever going to cope."

"And I'm grateful for that," he said, returning her affectionate gesture. "You spared me a year of misery. I'm not sure if I could've coped for that long."

"If I have anything to say about it, you won't have to," Mary said, "but therein lies the scary part. What we're doing here—what we're creating together—it's unknown territory for the both of us. Being an addict—especially a sex addict—really fucks up your concept of normal. The idea of being in love with someone, actually sharing my life with them and making myself vulnerable to them both emotionally *and* physically? It's just so different compared to how I've always done things."

"I see what you mean. Most of the women I hooked up with never told me their last name and I never bothered to ask. I never wanted to know someone that much. Even though we grew up together, the idea of knowing someone this well? Yeah, I guess that is kind of scary."

"Coming from a firefighter, that's saying something," Mary said, "but it helps make my point. We've done things one way, and sure, that way got us laid...a lot."

"Are you going to say that's a bad thing?" Peter asked.

"I wouldn't say it's good or bad. I'll just say we tried to get more out of it than we could and let it get so out of control that it nearly broke us. Well, now, we're taking a different approach—a more intimate approach."

She gave his hand a firm squeeze, conveying to him the love that had blossomed so much over the past few weeks. It made this brave, muscular firefighter tremble in her grasp. He didn't seem to mind, though. Mary had grown fond of the way he just held her, conveying to her the same evolving love.

"It'll still get us laid," Mary continued, "but that's not the endgame this time."

"It's still a nice bonus, though," teased Peter.

"That it is. It's also an ongoing process, one we'll have to figure out along the way. Being recovering sex addicts, it's bound to be more challenging. I imagine most newbie lovers don't have baggage like ours."

"I'm a firefighter, remember? I'm used to carrying heavy

loads. If you're willing to bear the burden, so am I."

"You say that with no hesitation whatsoever," commented Mary.

"You'd rather I hesitate?"

"Not at all. It's just that your steadfast certainty in loving me makes me want to love you even more."

Mary's words echoed with more passion than she'd expected. Then again, Peter Rogers had been defying her expectations in all sorts of ways. She was still getting used to that as well, but couldn't care less if she did.

Following that sentiment, Mary scooted a little closer to Peter so she could immerse herself in his warmth. He eagerly embraced her, slipping his arm around her waist and pulling her closer. He still had morning breath and she still had the kind of disheveled look that made her avoid mirrors. It didn't matter. Her passion for him overshadowed the reservations and vulnerabilities that had once held her back.

They drifted closer, naturally drawn together by their feelings. Mary was inches away from tasting his lips. Then a loud knock on Peter's door disrupted the moment.

"Were you expecting someone this early? Another passionate lover?" Mary said coyly.

"Ignore it. It's probably just that guy across the hall who keeps borrowing my towels," Peter said, clearly still eager to kiss her.

Mary felt inclined to take his advice. She leaned in again, but more knocking followed. This time, it was more urgent, indicating that ignoring it might not be an option.

"Damn. I better get that," Mary said with a sigh.

"You sure?" Peter asked.

"You made me breakfast. You let me borrow your shirt. The least I could do is answer your fucking door," she said playfully.

He didn't argue with her flawless logic. Mary, having to temper her passions for the moment, reluctantly pulled out of Peter's arms and got up from the table. He went back to eating his eggs while she made her way to the door, hoping this was someone she could tell to piss off so she could get back to her lover.

As she approached, Mary heard another round of urgent knocking. This time, however, a voice came along with it.

"Peter? Peter, are you in there? Please open up."

Mary froze for a brief moment, her hand just a few inches from the doorknob. She recognized that voice immediately. She also realized this was not someone she could just push away.

"Sister Angela?" she gasped. "Is that...?"

Mary got her answer before she could finish. As soon as she unlocked the door, the person on the other side pushed it open, and the next thing she knew, Sister Angela was standing right in front of her.

"Oh, dear God," the older woman gasped. "Mary?"

"Uh...hi, Sister Angela," replied Mary instinctively. "Um...what are you doing here this early?"

"You're in Peter Rogers' apartment, wearing his clothes, reeking of carnal sin and you're asking me what *I'm* doing here?"

Mary bit her lip to stop herself from responding in a way that would've made her more foolish. This might have been the most awkward moment she had ever experienced with clothes on. It wasn't just that she was now standing in front of a nun—her sex addiction counselor, no less—wearing only a pair of panties and a shirt that clearly wasn't hers. In seeing the older woman's worried eyes, she realized something that had completely slipped her mind and Peter's, for that matter.

In their effort to explore their new passions, they'd completely forgotten about Sister Angela and the Chapman Hill Addiction Outreach Program. She couldn't remember calling, texting or even mentioning her since that fateful night. It had left her and everyone else at the program to assume the worst.

Her presence—and the rather strident way Sister Angela

had addressed her — got Peter's attention. He immediately came over from the table, and as soon as he saw Sister Angela, he froze.

"Whoa. Uh…Sister Angela?" Peter said, now sharing Mary's awkward disposition. "This…isn't what it looks like."

"You're right, Mr. Rogers. This is *far* worse than I thought," said Sister Angela in a dire tone.

The older woman stormed farther into Peter's apartment, acting as though a demon were present. She barged past Mary and Peter, mumbling a series of prayers under her breath. Mary glanced over toward her lover, who had the same befuddled look on his face that he'd had in third grade when he'd forgotten his homework. They were both in an awkward situation. It had been bound to come up sooner or later, but it should've been sooner.

Sister Angela began pacing, praying and lamenting. She carried herself like a woman who'd just walked in on an unfolding disaster. She didn't know the context or circumstances of what had led to this newfound passion with Mary and Peter. That meant she had to assume the worst.

"This is my fault. After you didn't show up for your first-year ceremony, I knew something was wrong," she mused.

"Oh, yeah. I forgot about that," Mary said sheepishly. "I…was distracted."

"Sorry about that," muttered Peter.

"Don't you dare apologize," Mary said to him under her breath.

Sister Angela kept pacing. She looked on the brink of tears. Mary tried to approach her, but the older woman wouldn't stop panicking.

"I thought you needed space. I thought after Susan, you were…conflicted. I didn't want to push you. Pushing someone just before a milestone is rarely appropriate."

"You didn't push me," assured Mary. "You—"

Sister Angela didn't let her start. She just kept on pacing.

"I challenged you too much. I challenged Peter too much. You'd both worked so hard to put yourselves on the right path."

"It's not like that," Peter said.

"It's true. It's...actually not like anything you're probably thinking right now," added Mary.

It still didn't work. Sister Angela either wasn't listening or didn't hear them. She just kept pacing and praying, agonizing over this strange new development.

"I should've been more supportive of you, Mary. The first year of healing is always the hardest. This program fully acknowledges that."

"I appreciate that, but—"

"Please, let me finish," said Sister Angela, cutting Mary off again. "This relapse doesn't have to be a failure for either of you. It's perfectly normal to feel overwhelmed—even a bit empty at times. It's part of the struggle that we all endure on the road to recovery. That's why we need to keep praying—to support one another. It's the only way we can strengthen our souls. With a strong soul, we can overcome our addictive urges."

"I get that. I understand," Mary said, still trying to get a word in. "I just need to let you know that—"

It was no use. Sister Angela was on a roll.

"I'm not finished," she said, cutting Mary off once again. "I believe your soul is stronger than you think. I believe you have the strength to come back from this. You may not think it. You may not feel it. But it *is* there. I believe that strength is enough to overcome these urges."

"Yeah, about those urges—"

"I also believe you can become an inspiration to others—to everyone at the Chapman Hill Addiction Outreach Program. Your story doesn't have to end like Susan's. You can become living proof that through prayer and healing, even the worst addicts can achieve this strength."

"But I—" Mary said, now getting frustrated.

"I know you have doubts. You may even feel like you

haven't made much progress," the older woman continued.

"Sister Angela—"

"And I can say without reservation that you have. That progress doesn't have to disappear after this."

"Sister Angela—"

"I can also say you can become even stronger after this. I'll help you."

"Sister Angela—"

"I think that if you and Peter just came to the meeting tonight, we can—"

"Sister Angela! For God's sake, shut up and listen!" shouted Mary.

She hadn't meant to be *that* harsh, but she had to stop the woman. With every word, Sister Angela was making it harder on herself, as well as on her and Peter. A lot had changed since she and the nun had last spoken.

This also gave Sister Angela a moment to gather herself. She was still concerned, but she'd finally stopped pacing. She still kept looking at her and Peter with worry and dread. Mary wanted to be annoyed with her for barging in on such a pleasant morning, but she couldn't be too upset. The nun's heart was always in the right place and they had kind of forgotten about her. For that reason, Mary had to do this as carefully as possible. However, it might be best for both of them if she kept things simple and blunt.

"I'm sorry, Sister Angela. I know how this looks. Trust me. It's not as dire as it seems," Mary said calmly. "Yes, Peter and I relapsed, so to speak. If by that word, you mean we had sex, then, yeah, I guess that would qualify."

"You guess?" said Sister Angela, looking both skeptical and confused. "Mary, need I remind you that you and Mr. Rogers are addicts? An addict cannot and should not make light of a relapse."

"I *totally* agree. That's why we're not making light of it."

"She's right," Peter said, offering a gesture to assure the older woman. "Believe me, this may be the most serious, most meaningful development in our adult lives. It just happens to involve a relapse."

Sister Angela was still confused. Mary could hardly blame her. This probably defied every tenet and teaching of CHAOP. A relapse wasn't supposed to heal two self-professed sex addicts. It wasn't supposed to manifest in such a powerful, passionate way. God might move in mysterious ways, but some just defied understanding to those who hadn't experienced such passion.

"Don't start cursing yourself, Sister Angela. You didn't fail us. The program didn't fail us either—not entirely," Mary continued.

"How? How could you expect me to not blame myself?" said the older woman. "I worked with you, talked with you and prayed with you. We spent a whole year rebuilding your soul—a soul you admit was shattered by your addiction."

"It definitely was," affirmed Mary, "and you did help me put the pieces back together. The problem wasn't you. Your heart was in the right place. It always was, and I never doubted that."

"Me, neither," Peter said. "I haven't known you nearly as long, but from what Mary tells me, you've got a hell of a halo over your head."

"And you put it to good use," Mary said. "You show people like me—people who are so broken on the inside—what their addiction has done to them. You give us perspective, despite our addiction skewing damn near everything we think we know about ourselves."

"But perspective isn't enough," said Sister Angela, now calmer, but still very anxious. "For any addict to recover, they must learn restraint. I spent nearly a year with you, Mary—a year building your strength so you could resist your addictive urges."

"Therein lies the problem, Sister Angela. Restraint isn't— and *shouldn't*—be the endgame. I needed more to heal from the scars of my addiction. I needed something—no, *someone* more powerful."

Mary turned toward Peter, who was already smiling at her choice of words. She moved in closer to him and took his hand in hers. She gave it an affectionate squeeze, one that conveyed love and not just desire. She made sure Sister Angela saw it. That way, she could see the difference between a relapse and a revelation.

"In the year I spent at CHAOP, I learned a lot about myself, my problems and the others who share those issues," Mary continued. "Those lessons went a long way toward rebuilding some vital parts of my soul."

"She's been sharing those lessons with me, too," added Peter. "They really are powerful."

"That's all well and good, but no matter how much we learn about them…it doesn't really change anything," Mary went on. "Even after I rebuilt part of my soul and saw these scars, I didn't know how to fix them. Not acting on my urges didn't heal them. Talking about it didn't do it. Praying didn't solve it. In the end, I needed something else to complete that process."

"And you couldn't find it in the program or with my help?" asked Sister Angela.

"No. I couldn't because…it found me instead," Peter interjected.

As soon as he said the words, Mary put an arm around his shoulder and pulled him into a light, loving embrace. She tried to make it obvious that what they had done could not be mistaken for the actions of sex addicts undergoing a destructive event. Mary demonstrated as clearly as any divine revelation that what she'd done with this man had been no simple relapse. It was something so much more. It finally got Sister Angela to calm down to the point where she stopped lamenting. Now, she seemed genuinely curious.

The nun gazed at her and Peter as though they were holding some holy relic. She often reminded everyone at CHAOP that she had seen it all. She had witnessed the greatest depths of addiction and the greatest miracles of healing. However, Mary got the impression that she had never seen something like this.

Just being close to Peter, feeling his strong grasp and genuine warmth, she might as well be a whole, new person. That person still had problems, but she now had the tools and the passion to fix them.

"In my defense, I never intended to find her in that way," Peter said jokingly.

"I don't think either of us meant for this to happen. We knew each other as kids, we moved to opposite sides of the country and we became raging sex addicts of our own accord. For us to come together again all these years later, find each other in our darkest hours and just heal each other with such a passion..."

"A lot of passion, mind you," added Peter.

Mary laughed at his remark and gave him a playful swat. Sister Angela didn't share in the laughter, but she at least cracked a smile. Mary sensed the older woman was finally seeing what she and Peter had realized together.

"Call it fate. Call it destiny. Call it an act of God granting mercy on two broken souls," Mary said. "It happened. It worked. Sure, it involved us having sex again, but to call what we did mere sex?"

"Yeah, I think God can see the difference," Peter said confidently.

This time, Sister Angela did laugh. She obviously was starting to see the difference, too. It probably tested her faith. It probably tested a lot of what she thought she knew about treating sex addicts. Whether divine or not, the results spoke for themselves.

"Beyond the sex and how it happened — which, in and of itself, is pretty amazing — that passion revealed something else," Mary went on.

"I can appreciate revelations more than most, but I'm still struggling make sense of it all," Sister Angela said.

"To be honest, we haven't made complete sense of it, either, but we know enough to know it's right," Mary said confidently. "Every addict has scars to some degree—scars that drive us toward addiction or keep it going. Sometimes those scars aren't just there to remind us of the pain. Sometimes they tell us things—important things that both addicts and recovering addicts don't realize."

"Even when we try to listen, we don't make it easy on ourselves. In fact, we may even avoid it," Peter said.

"In the end, what they tell us still holds true. These scars didn't just fuel decadent desires. They suppressed good ones—meaningful ones that could fill the emptiness that addiction tends to create. I've found a way to embrace those desires with Peter…and I want to keep doing so."

"So do I," he said. "It doesn't always have to be when we're fully clothed, but they're so worth embracing."

Mary rewarded his kind yet crude words with another playful hug. It helped reinforce her special feelings for him. It wasn't just sexual. It wasn't simply pure passion, either. It was something so much more profound.

Sister Angela remained silent for a few moments. This clearly wasn't a part of her training with CHAOP or the vows she'd taken when she'd become a nun. This was uncharted territory for her as well as them. At least now she wasn't pacing and panicking, worried that this relapse was entirely a bad thing.

Mary didn't expect her to understand, but Sister Angela had always been good at listening to addicts like her. She genuinely wanted to help them in any way possible. This way was just so unusual.

After taking a few moments to process it all, the older woman cast her and Peter a curious gaze. For a moment, it felt like she was scrutinizing them, as if looking for any signs of sin. She must not have seen any because, in the end, she smiled. Whatever her experience and piety told her, Sister Angela could no longer deny what she saw in them.

"This…is an unexpected development, to say the least," said Sister Angela, sounding both relieved and conflicted. "This relapse, so to speak, certainly isn't as bad as I feared."

"Glad we convinced you of that," Peter said. "I don't think we should strain our souls more than we already have."

"I agree," said the older woman. "I suppose I should also apologize."

"Apologize? For what?" Mary asked, now offering the nun a reassuring gesture.

"For having too much faith in the program and not enough faith in those it serves," she said. "Long before I took my vows, I learned that we all must find our own way down the right path. Mine led me to a life of piety. I sometimes forget that not everyone is drawn to that path."

"I think God understands that, as well. I don't think we're all meant to be priests or nuns," Peter said.

"Yes, and we're not always sure of our own path, let alone others'. Perhaps CHAOP would be wise to remember that. I now fear that addicts like you will suffer far less profound experiences."

Her fear was not unfounded. Mary hadn't forgotten that she wasn't the only recovering sex addict in Hartman County. She hadn't forgotten that she'd spent nearly a year in this program, struggling to rebuild her life. It had been a difficult year, to say the least, but once Peter had entered her life, those struggles had felt worth it.

Looking back toward Peter, then at Sister Angela, she marveled at how far she had come. Peter gave her warm smile, reminding her that she wasn't the only one who had come the distance. That gave her an idea.

"Well, if you want...Peter and I could come to the next CHAOP meeting and share our experience," Mary said.

"Really? You still want to be part of the program?" said Sister Angela with renewed intrigue.

"We're still recovering sex addicts, remember? A few weeks of passion doesn't change that."

"And here I was thinking we'd skipped that part," Peter said.

"There's no skipping steps when you're in recovery. You taught me that, Sister Angela," Mary continued, "and if you think our fellow addicts could benefit from what Peter and I have discovered, we'd be happy to share it."

"Although we may have to censor a few parts," teased Peter.

"But don't worry," assured Mary. "We'll be sure to preserve the important stuff."

This time, Sister Angela didn't hesitate to smile. She didn't even need to say yes. It was obvious the nun now saw the power of what Mary had uncovered with Peter. Mary was willing and eager to share this experience, knowing it would resonate with anyone struggling with misguided passions.

She — Mary Ann Scott — no longer defined herself by what she lacked. She understood her mistakes. She understood the path that had led to this point. Now, she was ready to forge a new one. It certainly helped that she wouldn't be doing it alone.

Mary reveled in her lover's warm presence. He didn't need to say another word. He just slipped his arm around her waist, conveying to her the emotion that had finally healed their ailing souls. Together, she and Peter had confronted their heavy burdens. They'd achieved a new understanding of what had fueled them. And through a special kind of passion, they'd gained a strength that was greater than any addiction.

More books from
Totally Bound Publishing

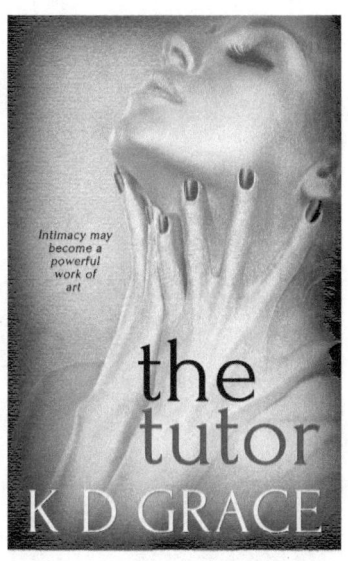

When physical touch is impossible, intimacy may become a powerful work of art or a devastating nightmare — but, above all, it's an act of trust.

Thrown into salsa lessons by her therapist, Fiona stumbles her way from depression to happiness and, numerous disasters later, finally finds her rhythm again.

Two hearts, both broken… Two lives ready to be lived.

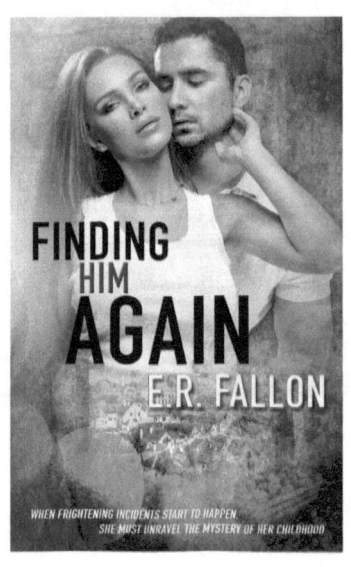

She came home to find the one romance she always regretted not having…

About the Author

Jack Fisher

Jack Fisher was born in Washington DC into a large, loving family that nourishes creativity at every turn. He grew up on a steady diet of comic books, movies, and Saturday morning cartoons. That diet gave him an active imagination, one he channelled into writing. He began writing at age 16 and hasn't really stopped since. He quickly developed a soft spot for romance, often writing fan fiction of his favourite fictional couples. Eventually, he graduated to writing stories about couples of his own creation, with a heavy focus on heated passion and powerful intimacy. He is currently single and lives just outside of DC. He is still a self-professed comic book lover and all around sci-fi geek while striving to refine his craft in any way he can.

Jack Fisher loves to hear from readers. You can find contact information, website details and an author profile page at https://www.totallybound.com/

Home of Erotic Romance

www.ingramcontent.com/pod-product-compliance
Lightning Source LLC
Chambersburg PA
CBHW020415180626
46812CB00003B/990